SEWING SUSPICION

A QUILTING COZY MYSTERY

KATHRYN MYKEL

Dragonfly's Press

Edited by Nancy Pile ZooWrite and Silvia Curry at Silvia's Reading Center
Proofread by Shari Oitzman at Sharp Eyed Shari and Nicole Zoltack
Beta Read by Nola Li Barr at Tapioca Press, Jessica Fraser, and Kirsten Moore at thebestbetareader@gmail.com
Cover Design by PixelSquirrel at www.etsy.com/shop/PixelSquirrel
Formatted by Nola Li Barr at Tapioca Press

This book is dedicated to Ernest LeBlanc—RIP.
This one is for you dad, we will read it together when we meet again.

Special thanks to all of my family, friends & peers. As well as all of the dedicated quilters; my fans and customers! I could not have done it without all of you.

STAY CONNECTED

For more fun content and new releases, join Kathryn on Patreon, sign up for her newsletter, or join her and her thReaders on Facebook at Author Kathryn Mykel or Books For Quilters.

authorkathrynmykelsewingsuspicion.mailerpage.com

CONTENTS

HOMECOMING

Drive safe and watch your back.
If you need me, call.

ALEX LOOKED DOWN AT THE TEXT FROM HAWK, A LOCAL private investigator, and reminded herself she was going home because her adoptive grandmother Nona was demanding it. Hawk was the only other person in her life who knew the true reason she was leaving New York City.

Single with no real attachments to the city besides her former condo and career, Alex had been ready when Nona called her home.

"Come home," Nona had uttered.

"Are you in trouble? What is this about?" Alex had asked.

"Just come. I need a lawyer ... I need you," Nona had pleaded, thinking about the threatening notes she had received.

Nona had thought the first note was a prank or that the mailman mixed up the mail. She hadn't taken it seriously until the second note had passed through the mail slot two days later.

. . .

YOU'RE GOING TO NEED YOUR LAWYER.

She was taking the second note more seriously.

I AM COMING FOR YOU! —LVR

Not aware that anything nefarious was happening on Spruce Street, Alex had just wanted to appease the matriarch. It was unusual for Nona to admit that she needed anything or anyone, so whatever was going on, Alex was going to handle it in earnest.

"Okay, I'll come home this weekend," Alex had told her then added a little white lie, "I have some time off anyhow, and it will be nice to enjoy the summer in Salem."

"Thank you. You are my best girl. You know that, Alex?"

"Yes, Nona," Alex had responded. "I love you too. Now, I have to go. I have a meeting with the partners." Her voice had wavered, and she hoped Nona hadn't picked up on it.

Nothing got past Nona, especially when it came to Alex. "Is everything okay?" Nona had asked, waiting while Alex hesitated for a beat.

That was a good question, but she hadn't seen the point in adding undue stress to Nona in her current agitated state. "Yes, everything is fine. There's nothing to worry about. I'll see you in a few days."

Alex had submitted her formal written notice to the firm two weeks prior and had handed it to Weitz personally. She'd even reiterated the message verbally just yesterday—she resigned. She quit. She was leaving. Permanently. How many ways could it be conveyed? She was done with everything the firm represented, and now she even held the excuse of going home to care for Nona, practically the only family in her life. It became apparent to Alex that leaving the firm might be the hardest negotiation she'd ever have to make.

Still anxious about the meeting with the partners, Alex stopped to read the company lines. They were scripted on a life-size placard bolted an inch away from the wall. Twice before she had made this long walk to the executive conference room— once when she had been hired and once when she had been given a permanent position and office in the Romano division.

The Law Firm of Weitz & Romano

The Weitz division of Weitz & Romano is responsible for mergers and acquisitions, antitrust litigation, and multi-billion-dollar real estate ventures.

The Romano division of Weitz & Romano is responsible for criminal defense, providing clients with the highest level of representation, with personal attention tailored to their clients' unique needs.

Alex pressed her hands from her jacket to her skirt, smoothing herself out even though her Armani suit wasn't wrinkled. She steeled herself and reached for the ornate bronze door handle.

"Take some time," Romano mused, leaning back in his chair.

Weitz flashed an icy smile as he said, "We understand."

The two partners had an annoying habit of volleying back and forth in conversation, finishing each other's thoughts and sentences, but Romano always gave the last word.

The way he made eye contact and lingered too long was uncomfortable. In this case, Romano dismissed her from the meeting. His final words were, "Family comes before all else."

Technically, she had resigned, but—shaking her head in disbelief on her way back to her office—they weren't going to let her go!

Alex shivered when she turned off the monitor on her desk and did a cursory inspection to make sure she wasn't leaving anything personal behind. All of her clients had been transitioned to other lawyers. They weren't happy about it, and she didn't think she was escaping untethered. Only time would tell. Would they honor her request to separate from the firm completely? Everything was in place for Alex to go home to Spruce Street, move back into her family home, and look after Nona.

She didn't have much to pack up on her last day. There were no mementos or weird molded clay things from kids sitting on the large ornately carved oak desk, just a single picture frame that housed two pictures.

One was a picture of her parents, the equivalent of a selfie and hashtag, that they'd emailed to her from a kiosk on board a cruise ship. The picture of her mom and dad had been superimposed on the side of the ship with a note that read, "Cruisin' '02

Miss you, honey. We'll see you in a few days." Alex winced and stroked the frame before putting it in her quilted messenger bag.

The other picture in the frame was of her and Nona when Alex had graduated the top of her class from law school. It had been an adventure getting Nona into New York, but Nona had made it through in typical Nona style. Over the course of just two and a half days, Nona had voiced an opinion about everything from traffic to trash collection. *They're doing it all wrong,* Alex could still hear in her mind. *That's the problem with the big city.* To her credit, Nona had complained about everything except Alex.

She remembered the day fondly. *You're my best girl,* Nona had whispered to her along with giving her a quick hug before she'd taken her seat to watch Alex get her diploma.

It had been one of many hard milestones in Alex's life without her parents, but Nona had been there for her. Nona never failed to be present when Alex needed her, and now Nona needed Alex.

Alex kicked off her heels and tied up her sneakers. She slid her pumps into her quilted messenger bag, put on her raincoat, and saddled her bag around her shoulder.

"Ten years ... nearly a hundred cases," she sputtered and left the office as if she had never been there.

2

A NEW CHAPTER

In only four hours, Alex would be back on Spruce Street. Her feelings about going home were mixed, but she was glad that Nona's need provided her with a good cover story. Not that she really needed one, but it would be easier than explaining what she suspected was going on at the law firm.

She smiled when she turned onto Main Street. She was taken back every time she came home. The scenery had changed over the years. New businesses opened and closed all over town, but several familiar businesses still dotted the street. The hair salon—A Better Cut; the café—Rise and Grind; and the quilt shop—Nuts & Bolts.

She clicked on her turn signal and pulled slowly onto Spruce Street, a cul-de-sac with houses in a crescent shape lining the left side of the street. Spruce Street was an odd street, quite literally. It was a town within the town of Salem, Massachusetts. A neighborhood with a unique blend of houses and residents—a handyman, a city clerk, a baker, and a grouch. Alex laughed at the thought. Spruce Street even contained the police, fire, and mayor, and, of course, a mother, Nona.

Just as she passed number 13, technically the first house on the street, the familiar neighborhood welcomed Alex with open arms. Her eyes took in every house at once. Numbered as they had been built over the years, the houses were odd numbered and out of order. And though she never truly understood why, her neighbors referred to all the houses by their number, not by who lived in them, or the usual "my house" or "our home."

Alex rolled down her window and took in a deep breath of spruce from the thick forest to her right, twenty acres with hiking and game trails as old as the town itself. She parked the rental in front of number 1, which was perched higher than the other homes atop a gentle hill. The three-story home, built first but positioned at the end, appeared to be overlooking the whole street, the mother to all the neighborhood, just like Nona.

After grabbing a couple of bags from the backseat, Alex climbed the timber steps. The familiar smell of lilacs drew her in. She dropped the bags and rambled up the lawn, fifty feet or so, to pluck a fresh sprig from one of the lilac bushes. Retrieving her bags, she carefully maneuvered the luggage around, so she didn't crush the lilacs, and trekked up the extra-wide porch.

Reaching for the antique door handle, Alex turned it and let herself in through the oversized front door. She didn't need her house key. No one ever locked their doors on Spruce Street. Alex dropped her bags in the entryway and put her keys in the crystal bowl. The bowl sat on a small quilted placemat on a pedestal table that had belonged to her great-grandmother.

She put the sprig of lilacs in the vase filled with other fresh flowers and called out, "Nona, Pam, Charlotte?" even though Alex saw Nona "nona-ing." Yes, she had her own verb. She'd been peering through the curtains in the window while she sat waiting for Alex in the living room.

When Alex turned the corner, she saw Nona relaxing in her recliner. She was hand-stitching her hexies for her latest Grandmother's Flower Garden quilt, the only quilts she ever made as far as Alex knew.

"Oh, I didn't realize you were here," Nona said, acting coy, but it wasn't going to fool anyone.

Alex just shook her head and laughed. "Nona, I have missed you." Alex leaned down to give her a peck on the cheek. "This is new," Alex said, petting the fancy silk handkerchief wrapped around Nona's hair.

"Ah, it's nothing." She swatted at Alex's hand.

"Should I start calling you 'Thelma' or 'Louise'?" Alex joked. "What's with the new attire?" Alex gestured to her own head, miming an explanation of her question. The oversized sunglasses sitting on the side table hadn't gone unnoticed either.

"Never mind that." Nona air-swatted, just missing Alex as she sat on the sofa.

"Where's Pam?" Alex asked. "And where's Charlotte? I thought they would be here today."

"Pam left."

"And Charlotte?" Alex urged.

Nona tried to dismiss the whole conversation by waving her hand. "Never mind where that girl is."

"That girl'?" Alex questioned. "Since when do you call your granddaughter 'that girl'?"

"Never mind her right now. You are my best girl, Alex."

"Yes, Nona. I am. I love you too. Now, tell me what have you done with Charlotte."

Nona chuckled. "What do you mean, 'what have I done with her'?" Nona tsked. "The way you make it sound! She's not here. Now let's get you settled," she said while gesturing upstairs.

"When is she going to be home?" Alex asked her squirrelly gran as they climbed up the stairs.

Once on the landing, Alex saw Charlotte's room was empty. No signs of Charlotte at all.

"Nona?" Alex demanded. "Where is Charlotte?" Alex dropped her bags on her sleigh bed. In her haste, her tote bag slid off, and everything fell out.

Nona stood there, gawking at Alex while she kneeled down and picked up the throng of personal items strewn across the floor.

"Charlotte moved out weeks ago."

Alex stood. Nona looked Alex right in the eyes, challenging her to argue with her, but it was late in the day, and Alex was tired.

Though Alex had updated her room from a teenager's room to a more modern room befitting an adult, it still gave her comfort. For a brief moment, she was transported back in time, three decades earlier when she had been a young girl and her parents had still been alive.

"Why did she move out, Nona? Please, start at the beginning and tell me the whole story." It was becoming increasingly annoying, getting only little snippets at a time out of her.

"She's too modern, with all her modern ways and thinking."

"What does that even mean?" Alex asked, shaking her head in further frustration.

"It was so easy to teach you to quilt, but Charlotte, she just refuses to do things the traditional way. She insists on her newfangled machine and those gadgets."

"Okay, let me get this straight. Charlotte moved out because she's too modern?" Alex bemused. She was beginning to feel she had landed in a cartoon and was being confronted by the Cheshire Cat.

"Well, you know how kids are these days," Nona remarked.

"Nona, Charlotte and I are the same age. Besides, Charlotte loves quilting nearly as much as you do. Never mind. I will call

Charlotte after dinner and get to the bottom of this." Alex stood, tilted her head at the octogenarian, and gave a deep smile. Alex didn't take Nona's antics to heart, but the conversation was far from over.

Ignoring her, Nona turned her back to leave. "Let's eat," she called on her way out. "I made some chop suey, your favorite comfort food." Her voice trailed as she made her way slowly down the stairs. "And Betty dropped off one of her famous pies."

After their incredible dinner, Alex brought in a few more bags under the watchful eyes of Nona.

"Why do you have so much stuff? You never bring this much," Nona asked.

Now it was Alex's turn in the hot seat.

Her first thought was one of defiance. *I'll play your little game of cat and mouse.* However, the loveseat welcomed her, and she sank into the mauve monstrosity and explained everything to Nona.

"The truth is, Nona, I am home to stay." Alex watched as Nona's complexion began to redden, and she folded her arms across her chest.

When Alex reminded her that Pam was going to be leaving to go home to care for her own parents, she saw deep sadness cross Nona's face, and her eyes glazed.

"We are all going to miss Pam; however, I am here now, and we are going to start a new chapter in our lives." As Alex said the words, her own eyes welled up. Alex reached for Nona's clenched hand. "I know this isn't exactly your plan, Nona."

Nona's posture softened as she squeezed Alex's hand, but the scowl on her face made it clear that she was going to need some time to adjust to the changes.

Though Nona never uttered a word, Alex felt compelled to make sure Nona was clear. "It is final. I have left the law firm, and I am here to stay," Alex said, as she leaned in to give her a gentle squeeze.

She was getting anxious about the lack of a two-sided conversation here. She gave Nona time to cool, or scheme, and she headed upstairs to call Charlotte.

She didn't know what Nona had done to make Charlotte leave, or if she ever would.

Alex had no reservations about letting Charlotte stay in the house. Even though it was Nona's *house* now, it would always be Alex's *home*. Alex was moved by Charlotte's thoughtfulness when she'd asked Alex for permission to move in while Charlotte was between jobs and boyfriends.

"It just didn't feel right moving back into my parents' house at my age," Charlotte had said when they'd last spoken.

"Of course, it's not an issue. Nona should be fine with it, but you should definitely talk to her about it before you do it," Alex had assured Charlotte.

Consequently, Alex had received a call from Nona in record time. Nona had plenty to say about her granddaughter moving into number 1, being between jobs, being between boyfriends, and about an hour's worth of other things to top off the list. Alex didn't understand why Nona behaved the way she did with Charlotte. Over the years, Nona had acted as if she truly was Alex's grandmother, her biological grandmother. Nona had read her books as a child. She'd told Alex fanciful stories about mysterious places, covert organizations, and hidden treasures. On the other hand, she tended to be aloof with Charlotte.

Alex had tried to set Nona straight, saying, "Nona, she's a

grown woman who needs a place to stay." She told Nona to get ready for Charlotte and at least try to be on her best behavior, but it was up to grandmother and granddaughter to do the rest.

"I was worried about you, Charlotte," Alex said over the phone to her friend. "Your room was empty, and all Nona would say was that you were too modern."

"Yes, that's her current problem. I am too modern. I guess because I won't conform to her old lady ways," Charlotte teased.

"I don't want to get in the middle of you two. I was just worried about you, and Nona was pretty tight-lipped about the whole thing."

"Of course, because it is foolish. Have you ever heard of a grandmother ostracizing her granddaughter for being too modern?" Charlotte pleaded.

"No, it does sound far-fetched, even for Nona's standards," Alex responded. "Something else must be going on."

"Wait, why are you on Spruce Street, Alex?" Charlotte questioned.

"I came home for good. I just broke the news to Nona. Seeing as Pam is going to be heading back to New Jersey to care for her own parents, I decided it was what I wanted to do."

"I would've stayed to look after Nona had I known," Charlotte said, apologetically.

"Oh, I know, Charlotte. It wasn't that. It was time for me to leave the city."

Alex wasn't going to worry Charlotte by mentioning that Nona had summoned her before Alex had even known why she had been summoned. She wondered if it had something to do with Charlotte.

Changing the subject back to Charlotte and Nona, Alex asked, "Why do you say she ostracized you? What else did she do?"

"She told me I was no longer welcome in her house and at her quilting meetings. In addition to that, she said she would talk to Sue, at the quilt shop."

"And tell her what? That you are too modern?"

"Yeah, I guess. I don't know. She gets wackier every year. I mean, I love her. She's my grandmother, but there's only so much..." Charlotte trailed off.

"I was going to head over to Nuts & Bolts tomorrow for some retail therapy. I will talk to Sue while I'm there."

"Good luck. You're going to need therapy now that you're back here," Charlotte joked, and they both had a good laugh.

"Okay. I'll try to get to the heart of it. However, Nona's not speaking to me right now either," Alex stated.

"How long have you been home, Alex?"

"Two hours."

3

RETAIL THERAPY

Alex resolved to get to the bottom of Nona's drama the next morning because she still didn't know why Nona needed a lawyer. She was fiddling with the binding of her quilt when she noticed a small stain on the corner of it. It was the last quilt her mom had made for her before she'd died. It was her princess quilt, named such because her dad had declared it to be, and the name had stuck. It was a wonky star quilt pattern in pink, purple, and teal fabrics. It was the only accoutrement that didn't match the new modern decor of her bedroom. Alex hadn't had the heart to put the quilt away. As she fell asleep, she made a mental note to pick up some Grandmother's Secret Spot Remover at the quilt shop tomorrow.

In the morning, Alex dressed and headed down for a hearty breakfast and to talk to Nona.

"Nona? Pam?" Alex called out. There was no sign of either.

Well, that explains why it is so quiet this morning.

Alex had slept in, which was rare for her. She'd woken to the little birds trilling outside her window. In the city, she'd burned the candle at both ends and would wake up much earlier to the city's particular early-morning sounds—air brakes from buses, the tinkling and clickets from the wheels of bicycles, and the chatter of people passing by on the street. All of which drowned out the sounds of the avian community.

It is going to be such a relief settling into this quieter, slower pace and catching up on my beauty sleep.

Alex grabbed her quilted messenger bag and keys. She loved the bag, but it was beat. The handles were all frayed and the batik designs at its base were nonexistent. She didn't really need such a big bag anymore. It had been the last project she and Nona had worked on before Alex had gone off to law school. Nona hadn't really worked on it, more like *snoop-ervised* the construction of it. Maybe a new bag and a new project would be just the thing for the two of them.

She pulled up at Nuts & Bolts Quilt Shop on Main Street, just a half mile from Spruce Street. Walking through the front door, she found the owner, Sue, working at the cutting counter.

Sue greeted Alex by name with a bright smile. "Hi, Alex, it's great to see you." Alex's face showed surprise when Sue followed with, "Nona was already here."

Sue was a good-looking woman, much taller than Alex. She sported a bob haircut that just kissed her shoulders whenever she moved her head. Every strand of her brunette hair was perfectly in place unlike Alex's cocoa-colored wavy mane that she had haphazardly thrown up in a messy bun.

"She told me you were home from the 'big city.'" Her hands moved up in air quotes for "big city."

It really shouldn't have been a surprise to Alex. "Yes, that's right," Alex confirmed and continued, "Before I forget, I need to get some Grandmother's Secret Spot Remover. Do you carry that?"

"Of course. I have some right here at the checkout counter," Sue said, placing a bottle on the counter.

"Did she mention Charlotte?" Alex asked.

"Oh, yes. You know how she is," Sue said, grinning a brilliant smile.

"I do," Alex agreed, eyeing the striking batiks in front of her with multi-colored dragonflies stamped on them.

Overhead, she heard a video playing on the TV, a documentary on batiks being made in Indonesia. Alex marveled as she watched men making the big copper stamps called TJAPs. The men twisted copper strips into designs and then soldered them to metal bases. The video showed the technique of wax-resist dyeing, where they dyed the fabric once, stamped the waxed design across the fabric, and then dyed it again. In the end, the wax was boiled off, and the large hunks of fabric were laid out across the lawn to dry in the sun.

"I just got here yesterday, and I already need some *retail* therapy." Alex put the stress on the word "retail" and chuckled.

"Well, that sure is a gorgeous batik you've got there. Just came in this week." Sue pointed to the fabric Alex had been petting unconsciously.

"Yes, I'll take two yards," she replied, "and I'm looking for a tote bag pattern. Nothing too big. I will use it as a purse, but it will need to fit some work files as well. I need to replace my messenger bag," Alex said, holding up the beat-up bag.

"Sure, I have just the pattern for you," Sue said. "How about this Fuji Tote by Purple Plum Patterns?" Sue suggested. "It will show off this batik very nicely. You can make it up pretty quickly. Pick out a couple coordinates for it," she said, pointing to a wall of fabrics in every color of the rainbow.

"Would you make me a kit with everything I will need?" Alex asked.

In her perpetually positive style, Sue replied, "Yes, of course."

"I will still take the two yards of the batik for my stash."

"Perfect," Sue responded.

Alex figured this was a good time to question Sue, while she was distracted, buzzing around the shop, getting everything Alex needed for the bag.

"What did Nona say about what was happening with Charlotte?" Alex asked as casually as she could, trying not to sound like a lawyer interrogating a witness.

"Oh, you know how she is. She was going on about her being too modern. I have no idea. I just bobbed my head and heard her out while I was cutting her fabric." Sue went on without being prompted. "She actually told me that Charlotte wasn't to come to any more of her quilting group meetings. Seemed a little extreme to me."

"Yes, me too," Alex murmured. "I was thinking it might be nice for Charlotte and me to reconnect and maybe come in and take a class together. Maybe attend some of the guild meetings here at the shop?"

"Oh, that would be great." Sue beamed. "You and Charlotte will fit right in with the other women in the group. They are all much closer to our age than Nona's group of..." Sue smirked and winked at Alex.

Alex snickered. Sue didn't have to finish the sentence. Alex knew Sue was referring to the "biddies." Alex was amused that Sue knew the inside tease about the "youngins" and the "biddies." When she thought about it that way, it sounded a little *West Side Story* in her head.

Sue rang up Alex's purchase. "Here's a class schedule and brochure about the guild meeting."

"Thank you," Alex said, as she made her way out. She stashed the bag in the SUV and headed for the Rise and Grind Café, located just across the street.

Well, that puts that to rest, Alex thought to herself. Sue had confirmed that both Alex and Charlotte were welcome to the shop and the quilting group, regardless of Nona's need to try to oust Charlotte.

4

RIGHT BEHIND YOU

As she entered the café, she was instantly greeted with a delicious mix of the aromas of baked goods and coffees.

Stepping up to the counter, the barista greeted her with a smile, a pleasant hello, and "What can I get for you today?" According to the name tag on his shirt pocket, his name was Joey.

Alex ordered a small hot chocolate with no whipped cream. "No need for the extra calories." Hot chocolate was an indulgence, especially here. It was delectable. Under the lid, if she removed it quickly, she would find a swirl of white chocolate in a fancy shape. Her stomach growled, and Joey looked up at her expectantly. "You had better give me a breakfast sandwich as well." She said and added, "To go."

As she was about to remove the lid to see the surprise inside, she heard a familiar squeaky voice behind her, Betty Rekorc, infamous pie maker and neighborhood busybody, Nona's long-time best friend from Number 7 Spruce Street.

"Hi, Betty," Alex said, turning to greet Betty with an arm hug.

Betty leaned in and said, "We are so glad to have you home, Alex."

We? Who's 'we'? The mouse in her pocket?

Assuming Betty meant herself and Nona, Alex wasn't sure *how* Nona was handling the news because Alex hadn't seen her since she'd delivered it.

"Did you come home because of that incident last week?" Betty asked, using all her theatrics on the word "incident," widening her eyes and feigning innocence.

Alex stepped back in surprise. "What incident?"

"She had such a fright. I'm so glad she has a panic alert button and wasn't hurt, being home alone, with Pam away for the weekend and Charlotte already moved out. I got one of those panic systems too. You can never be too careful. It might be high time everyone starts locking their doors on Spruce Street when someone can just waltz in, in the middle of the night, and vandalize your home."

Betty seemed genuinely disturbed, though this was the first Alex had heard of this. *Panic alert system? Why hasn't Nona, or Pam, or anyone told me about this?*

Alex leaned in, and Betty took a sharp breath. "The Real Life Alert company called the police station when Nona didn't answer the phone. Officer Mark was sent to rescue her. You can imagine how that went ... you know, Mark showing up when Nona was in nothing but her nightgown. She didn't even tell Pam about what happened," Betty replied as if she had read Alex's thoughts.

Well, that explains that, but what was vandalized?

"Whoever broke in, Nona didn't see. The person just slammed a few doors, knocked a few pictures off the wall, broke a vase of flowers, and made a mess," Betty noted, answering Alex's internal question again. "Nona said the house had a weird smell, like fruit. Strange. The craziest story I've heard in a while, and I hear a lot of crazy stories." She took a much bigger breath this time, preparing for the next volley of information.

Alex continued to let Betty talk uninterrupted. As a lawyer, she had two modes—interrogate and listen. Listening was the best way to deal with people who liked to talk too much.

"And I am sure you heard about Jack and his new wife, Jennifer," Betty chattered.

So, Nona has bent Betty's ear about that too. Of course.

"You just missed her, Jennifer," Betty said, waving her hand at the door, and Alex's eyes followed.

"I didn't talk to her," Betty continued, grabbing Alex by the arm as she pulled her to a nearby table. The barista followed with Alex's breakfast sandwich.

"Thank you, Joey."

"My pleasure, ma'am."

Even though there was only one other person in the café, Betty ducked her head and leaned closer to Alex to whisper. "Did you know Jack met Jennifer in Las Vegas, and they got married ... in Las Vegas ... after knowing each other for just a few days?"

Alex didn't have to feign shock. She felt it in her bones. She knew Jack had gotten married, and that it was quick, but she hadn't known the sordid details. Besides, it wasn't any of Alex's or Betty's business, but Betty continued to blabber anyway.

"And she has a dog too! Kibbles. Who names their dog after its food?" Betty continued without taking a single breath. Her bulging eyes and the look of disdain on her face were almost too much for Alex. She had to hold back a laugh.

"Oh, I met *that* Jennifer when they first got to town. I made them a cherry pie," Betty added with a wink.

Alex did not lose the double meaning. Of course, Betty had made a pie, no doubt just as an excuse to get the gossip.

"She's not a bright girl, that Jennifer. I am pretty sure those boobs of hers are fake too. What was Jack thinking? Marrying someone not much older than his own daughter?"

21

Alex's mouth dropped, but she quickly recovered. She couldn't believe what Betty was saying. Alex had been in town less than twenty-four hours, hadn't been actively involved in the neighborhood in many years, and here was Betty telling her all the sordid details, details that Nona should have clued her into by now.

Alex wanted to stop her, but Betty was on a roll, and Alex was enjoying watching Betty relay her gossip. With each bit of information, her facial expressions were amplified, and Alex wouldn't even be sure how to describe what Betty was doing with her eyebrows. Besides the comicality of it all, it was a much quicker way to get information. Alex wouldn't have to interrogate Nona about it later. Betty gossiped, but she never embellished the stories.

Her eyes were bright, and she flashed a dazzling smile at Alex. "Nona came by this morning. We had a bit of apple crumb cake. She told me you have come home for good. Nona was beaming with pride to have you home."

I wonder if she has false teeth? Alex pondered as Betty bleated on.

"She also demanded that Charlotte was out, out of the group. It seemed a little absurd to me, but far be it for me to meddle," Betty noted with a shrug.

At that, Alex just couldn't resist laughing, as she repeated to herself Betty's words, *Far be it for you to meddle, Betty.*

"What's so funny?" Betty asked.

Alex was about to brush it off when Betty began *again.* "Nona has been festering about this situation with Jack and Jennifer." Betty leaned in closer, as if she was about to tell Alex a secret. "Truth is, we have been having apple crumb cake every morning for over a week now, ever since he came home with that ditzy broad." When Alex scowled, Betty added, "Nona's words. Not mine," and sat back, putting her hands up in defense.

Alex was used to letting nothing show in the courtroom, like a stone, but here in her hometown, sitting across from the town busybody who was dishing out the neighborhood gossip, with Nona the instigator at the center of the whole thing, and Alex not knowing any of it—it was working on her last nerve with Nona. She was glad she had run into Betty this morning after all.

"Alex, are you listening?" She paused. "I was saying that Nona wants to cut Jack out of the will. Probably why she wanted you to come home this weekend." Betty inclined her head toward Alex.

Now we're getting somewhere.

"I don't really know about this will that she was going on about. Everyone knows the house is yours, so what else does she have?" Betty asked and silently stared at Alex.

"I don't know either, Betty. In fact, I was looking for Nona this morning."

"Oh, she went to the salon to have her hair done. We normally all go on Friday afternoons. Nona goes nearly every day now."

"Well, thank you, Betty. I have a bunch of errands to run this morning. No doubt I'll be seeing you." Alex muttered, "Often," under her breath and smiled politely.

She squeezed Betty's hand, rose from the table, dropped her cup and cold uneaten sandwich in the trash by the door, and exited as quickly as possible.

Well, I am not going to follow Nona to the hair salon. I will have to wait until she gets home. Besides, I have a stain to tackle.

5

MS. FIX IT

BACK ON SPRUCE STREET, ALEX BROUGHT THE QUILT downstairs to the kitchen sink to try to remove the stain. She read the directions on the little bottle of Grandmother's Secret Spot Remover with the cute little granny on the front.

Just a spray is all it takes, the little bottle read. *Spray it right on the spot, wait 5 to 10 minutes, and hand or machine wash as normal.*

While she waited for the little granny's magic elixir to do its job, she made additional space for herself in the spare room. It would serve well to hold her boxes and furniture, and once she was settled, it would be perfect for a sewing room and office area for her to work out of.

She could still see the little brown villain. It was no larger than a dime, but it was there nonetheless. Alex put the stained corner of the quilt under the faucet to rinse, but the stain was still there. "Dratz," she mumbled. *Stain Maid next. Surely, Sue has*

other cleaning products at the quilt shop. She folded the quilt over one of the kitchen chairs to air-dry.

Alex pondered the situation about the will and the break-in. There was so much going on that Alex was in the dark about. *Why hadn't Nona told me what was going on? What was the point in withholding it all?*

As for the will, as far as Alex had known, no one in town knew how much money Alex had, nor that she had left Nona in charge of a large sum of it. It was Alex's money, but it was available to Nona to use as she saw fit, for herself, for her family, or for the neighborhood. Surely, she would have told Alex if she'd had a will drawn up with another lawyer? As far as Alex knew, there was no will, so why would Nona go around telling people there was? And why would she flaunt it? Alex was feeling even more troubled by Nona's behavior.

She heard the door downstairs and decided it was time to find out what all this nonsense was about. She stopped at the top of the stairs to listen to the commotion.

"Alex will get this all straightened out," she heard Nona saying.

Alex could hear Pam's voice too but couldn't make out what her responses were to Nona's erratic conversation. Alex coughed to signal her approach, and Nona looked up the stairs at her. Nona's blonde wavy hair, that should have been fresh from the hair salon, was a mess. Her usually put-together glamorous look—a stylish two-piece matching top and pants outfit—had seen better days. She was misbuttoned, and it even appeared as though she had on mismatching socks—one white and one pale pink.

"I know you will take care of everything, Alex," said Nona.

Alex eyed her speculatively "Yes, Nona, I surely will, but you first need to tell me everything that's going on."

As Nona began to speak, Charlotte tapped on the door and

let herself in. She stopped quickly inside the door, surprised to see everyone standing there in the foyer.

Nona snarled, "What is she doing here?"

"I just came to check on you," Charlotte responded.

"Your ears must've been ringing, Charlotte. We were just about to find out what has been going on here with Nona," Alex noted.

"Not with her here." Nona pointed a gnarly arthritic finger in Charlotte's direction.

Ignoring Nona, Charlotte peered directly at Alex and said, "I'll go. I don't want to upset her."

"No, you stay, we need to get to the bottom of this," Alex demanded. "Nona, just be straight. Tell us what is going on with you."

"I am writing that no-good son of mine out of my will. That's why I asked you to come this weekend."

"What will, Nona?" Alex asked.

"Well, fine, there's no actual will, but we will make one, so I can write that no-good son of mine out of it," she paused. "And my granddaughter too."

And her little dog too? Alex mused. "Nona, what has happened to make you so upset?"

"Ornery," Charlotte scoffed. "If there is no will, then you can't write me out of it. Besides, what are you going to take from us, number 9?" Charlotte referenced her childhood home and smirked, knowing she had won the argument.

"Well, I hadn't thought about that, but yeah," Nona replied and snickered like a rebellious teenager.

"Now, Nona, you know that number 9 is Jack's house. I helped you with the transfer of ownership two years ago," Alex added.

"I won't let a Las Vegas hussy get anything of mine," Nona snarled.

"What did Jennifer do to you? Dad is happy with her," Charlotte stated.

"I don't want to talk about it in front of her anyway," Nona said, pointing a witch-like finger at Charlotte again.

"It's fine," Charlotte responded, throwing her hands up. "I'll go. You can deal with this." She waved her hand, referencing Nona. She was clearly at her wits' end.

Charlotte stormed off, and Pam excused herself with an apologetic shrug. It was up to Alex now to figure this out.

"She's a bimbo with those fake Las Vegas boobs," Nona commented.

"Nona," Alex nearly yelled, "this isn't like you. Do you have a valid argument against Jack and Jennifer?" She couldn't help her inner lawyer surfacing.

"Ha, did you hear that?" Nona scoffed. "Jack and Jennifer. It even sounds terrible!"

"What? Okay, now you are just being ridiculous, Nona."

"And her little dog too!" Nona shouted.

Alex had to laugh at *The Wizard of Oz* reference that had already come to her earlier in the conversation.

"Charlotte thinks Jack is happy with Jennifer. Why are you so upset about it?"

"Alex, you left me with a lot of money. I tried to do good with it over the years. If anything happens to me, I don't want it to fall into that evil money grubber's hands." Nona stared at Alex, pleading with her.

"Nona, please stop talking like this. It's out of character for you."

"I know," Nona resigned and plopped herself into her favorite loveseat.

Alex settled down beside her. "Okay, look, I've told you. The money is yours to leave to Jack and Charlotte if you choose to. There's more than enough to go around. Nevertheless, there is no way for Jennifer to get hold of it." She cupped Nona's hands in her own. "If you are worried about the money, we can draw up a will to specify exactly what you want. We can work on finding a solution to the problem here." Alex gave Nona's hands a gentle squeeze of assurance. "Now, do you have any valid reason to think the way you do about Jennifer?"

Nona hesitated, and Alex could swear she looked over toward her bedroom. Alex turned her head, but she didn't see anything out of the ordinary.

"Just look at her, with her bouffant hair, tight pants, fake boobs, and fake pink nails, and she smells sickly sweet. You can tell she is a gold digger," Nona harrumphed. "Who does she think she is, Olivia Newton John?" She wrenched her hands from Alex's. "She must think Jack has money. You know, sometimes he's boastful in those flashy suits of his." Abruptly, she stood up and put her hands to her hips.

Truth be told, Alex had told Jack about the money. Alex had wanted Jack to know she was taking care of his mother and where she was getting the money from. It was entirely possible, a huge stretch but possible, that he could have mentioned something about money to Jennifer.

"Well, I haven't even met her yet, Nona, and you can't make that judgement based on her hair, boobs, and nails."

The mood lifted, and they both began to hoot with laughter.

Thinking this was a good chance to bring up the incident, Alex asked, "What's been going on here, Nona? Betty mentioned an incident, a break-in. Why didn't you tell me?"

"Oh, it was nothing. Betty shouldn't have mentioned it. I can handle myself. It was probably just some kids causing a ruckus," she replied, dismissing the whole thing.

"I want to help, but you have to be straight with me, Nona. Did Officer Mark investigate?"

"Of course not. It wasn't even an incident," she baulked.

"Officer Mark, coming into a lady's bedroom when she's in nothing but her nightdress, that was the incident!"

"Scandalous," Alex gasped and put her hand to her mouth. She continued, glaring at Nona, "Someone broke in! That qualifies as more than an incident to me." Alex's tone grew sharper, and she began to pace the room. "You were only alone for two days!" she pointed out, throwing her hands in the air.

"It's not a break-in when the doors are unlocked."

"It sure the heck is!" Alex was much louder than she'd intended. "I'm sorry. I didn't mean to yell at you. I'm shocked you are not taking this seriously."

"Oh, I am taking it seriously. Why do you think I called my lawyer?" Her expression was serious all right as she gaped at Alex.

Alex cut her losses. She wasn't going to win this round. "At a minimum, we need to start locking the doors."

"Sure, sure."

There was no sense in arguing it further. She hoped Nona had gotten the message.

"Look, about Jennifer, how about I go over and meet her after dinner tonight? I am sure she is not a gold digger, as you call it."

"You will see. She is. I just know it. Something isn't right about that woman." Nona jabbed her finger in the air, making her point.

"Jack is the mayor. He wouldn't be fooled. He has a reputation to uphold," Alex assured, mostly for Nona's convincing but partially for her own too.

"Fake boobs and L-O-V-E. Oh, he *would* be fooled," she mocked.

Alex couldn't help but giggle. Sometimes, it was like she was the one raising Nona now. *The roles certainly are reversing.*

"It's just such a big responsibility, with all that money and all," Nona floundered.

"I am sorry, Nona. I didn't mean for it to be a burden on you," Alex said, rubbing the bridge of her nose to her eyebrows.

"No, no, child. It isn't a burden. I am so happy to have been able to help the neighborhood all these years. I've done amazing things with the money." She glanced up at Alex with a coy smile. "I think I've let my emotions carry me away lately," she confessed, "but maybe it is time for you to take the money back, so you can start using it. I am not getting any younger, you know."

"Speaking of younger people, what is going on with you and Charlotte?" Alex asked.

"You know, she just won't listen. She doesn't want to have anything to do with my 'old-fashioned quilting ways.' Her words."

"Nona, you know Charlotte loves quilting nearly as much as you do. It shouldn't matter if she is learning modern techniques."

"I wish she was more like you, Alex."

Alex stomped her foot, realizing a little too late that she was starting to behave like Nona. "Look, it is not fair to me or Charlotte for you to compare us. She is your granddaughter, and I know you love her."

"You are like a daughter to me, Alex."

"I know, but Charlotte and I grew up together. We were like sisters when we were younger. I am sure it wasn't easy on her all these years, watching you dote on me." Alex paused to collect her thoughts. "The art of quilting helped me heal and overcome the loss of my parents." Alex reached for Nona's hand again. "But my quilting journey was of necessity. Mine was a healing journey." Alex's eyes watered as the memories flooded her system. "Charlotte's quilting journey is different, Nona. It isn't the same for her. It is something she loves for the sake of the craft, something you both have in common and can share together."

"It is no wonder you are such a good lawyer, with all these speeches you like to give," Nona interrupted.

"You need to apologize to Charlotte, and I will stop over to number 9 later to meet Jennifer. Now let's go get Pam, and we'll sit on the porch and have some iced tea." She clasped Nona's hand in her own. "Rather than fighting, let's make the most of Pam's last few days with us." Alex gave Nona a winning smile to beat all smiles.

"Oh, Alex, I just can't believe she is leaving. It tears me up inside," she said with a sob.

Here we go again.

"I know, but I am here. It is the start of a new chapter." Alex gently rubbed Nona's shoulder. "Nona, are you sure there isn't anything else going on that I should know about?" Alex studied her eyes, trying to get a sense of what she was hiding.

"No, no," Nona replied and called upstairs for Pam.

Alex wasn't fooled. She knew Nona about as well as Nona knew herself, or at least up until this week, she had thought she did. Here, she could see right through Nona's facade. She was hiding something. Alex just didn't know what it was yet.

"Pam, let's pour a few glasses of iced tea and relax on the porch for a while," Nona suggested, as she stood up to compose herself.

"Yes, I think that will do you some good," Alex said to Nona and gave a hopeful nod to Pam.

"Don't start treating me like a poor little old lady," Nona demanded, and just like that she was back to her no-nonsense Nona self again.

Alex took a deep breath of fresh warm air. Though the summer had been mild as New England summers went, Alex had to admit the house was getting stuffy with all the windows shut. As they got themselves settled into the rocking chairs, Alex noticed a delivery truck stopping at Jack's house.

"She sure does get a lot of deliveries," Nona commented.

"Oh, Alex, don't get her started on the delivery trucks," Pam said with a grimace.

To change tack, Nona had fun with Alex instead. She spent the afternoon telling Pam about all of Alex's most embarrassing moments over the years. Together, they spent hours on the front porch reminiscing, telling stories, and laughing, snuggled under quilts until the sun went down.

6

MEETING MRS. LAS VEGAS

ALEX SPENT THE ENTIRE DAY PUTTERING AROUND IN HER rooms, unpacking and arranging the boxes of belongings that she had brought. The house had been filled with a rich aroma all day, and when her mouth started to water, she went down to investigate.

"Are we expecting company?" Alex asked as she lifted the lid on the Crock-Pot to expose the pot roast dinner cooking within.

Pam shooed her away. "It's ready. Go set the table," she said, "for three."

Alex dug into a hearty bowl of roast with potatoes, onions, and carrots. Pam's cooking was even better than Nona's, though Alex would never say it aloud.

After the three women had an uneventful dinner, Alex set out to head over to number 9 to meet "that woman." Alex was sure Jack knew what he was doing. He was a good judge of character. If he had fallen in love with Jennifer quickly, who were they to judge him for it? Alex reminded herself to be open-minded about the whole situation.

At the door, Jack greeted her with a huge bear hug and

invited her in. "We were just about to have some cherry pie. Join us, will you?"

Alex had to catch herself at the cherry pie reference again. She didn't want to be rude by laughing out loud. "Yes, that sounds great, Jack."

"This is my wife, Jennifer," he announced, beaming with pride as he introduced her.

Well, Nona was right. Bouffant hair, tight pants, clearly fake boobs, and those nails were something all right. She could see how this would set off alarm bells for Jack's traditional old-school mother. Jennifer was beautiful and young. Alex thought she resembled Peg Bundy, though she could now understand Nona's reference to Olivia Newton John's character from the movie *Grease*.

"So glad to meet you." Alex extended a hand, but Jennifer stepped close with her arms extended for a hug. It wasn't a very genuine hug, one of those pat hugs where you barely touched. Alex couldn't help herself and sniffed as she leaned in, but Jennifer didn't smell overly sweet as Nona had commented.

"I've heard so much about you, Alex. Come in. Let's have some pie."

So far, Alex's first impression of Jennifer seemed nice enough, if a bit fake too, and what was up with her hair? That aside, there were no red flags.

"I'd like it if you joined us at number 1 for the next quilt meeting. Do you sew or quilt?"

"Not really, Alex, but I could try to learn."

They enjoyed Betty's cherry pie with some light conversation until Jennifer excused herself, leaving the room to take a call. "It's my brother, I have to take this."

Alex had a nagging feeling like she knew Jennifer, but she was sure she'd never met her before. She would've remembered that hair. She had a photographic memory when it came to people's faces.

Alex and Jack chatted about the house, about the neighborhood and how she was settling in. She was just about to ask Jack about the incident with Nona when Jennifer came back into the kitchen looking horrified, like she had just received some really bad news.

"Is everything all right?" they asked in unison.

Composing herself, she walked to Jack's side, "Oh, yes, I'm fine. Nothing to worry about." Jennifer reached for a loaf pan on the stove and handed it to Alex. "Here, for Nona. I was going to bring it by later, but since you are here ... It's a spiced tea loaf. I made it myself."

Alex shook her head as she ambled up the steps to number 1 with Jennifer's tea loaf. She could see Nona peeking through the curtains. Nona was acting more like busybody Betty. *That's a tongue twister.*

The air was nice and cool, and she hesitated before going inside. She wanted to plop down on the porch swing and just sit for hours, like she had done when she had been younger and hadn't a worry in the world. Alex was exhausted after being back on Spruce Street for less than two full days, and now she still had to deal with Nona, one more time, before the day was done.

The instant Alex opened the door, Nona started in on her. "See? I knew you would see it too! I was right, wasn't I?"

"Nona, give me a minute. Let's sit. I am so full from Betty's cherry pie."

"You had pie with her?"

"Nona, stop. Yes, I ate pie with *them*. Jennifer was nice." Nona opened her mouth to start in on Alex, but Alex put a hand up to shush her. "Let me finish. Yes, her hair could be described as bouffant. Yes, her boobs appeared to be fake, way too perky even at her age, and I have no idea what the point of those nails is." Alex shivered. They certainly could do some damage.

"They're called daggers. The shape is called dagger. Pam searched it on the internet," she said proudly, still standing there in front of Alex with her hands on her hips.

"Sit, Nona," Alex said, sitting and patting the loveseat.

"I am not a puppy, Alex."

"Look, okay, so the shape of her nails is called daggers. I wouldn't wear mine like that," Alex said, looking down at her distressed French manicure. "But that doesn't mean she's a gold digger. You said dagger, not digger," said Alex with a silly face to try to lighten the mood. "She was pretty flighty, so I'm not sure she has much in the way of smarts, but I invited her to the quilt meeting."

"You did what?" Nona shrieked and then got up and began huffing and puffing around the room like a turkey in full plume. She paused and glared at Alex. "I thought you would be on my side."

"Nona, I think you are being ridiculous. She sent over this spiced tea loaf. I will serve us a slice, and we can have some calming tea. Then I am going to bed. No more talk of this

Jennifer nonsense tonight. We can talk about the will and the money and go over everything tomorrow." Alex got up and went into the kitchen to make tea.

Nona gave her the stink eye and, with arms crossed in an act of resistance, followed Alex into the kitchen. They sat at the dining table, and Alex served up two slices of the tea loaf. Nona didn't touch the tea or the slice of loaf cake.

"It really is very good," Alex teased, as Nona sat scowling across the table. "The tea too." She raised her cup in the air at Nona.

"Yeah, the tea is good but it is too sweet. It's from Jennifer also," she said begrudgingly. "Pam's been making it all week. Some special blend from Las Vegas. As if they make tea there," she griped.

"They can make tea anywhere, Nona," Alex said, as she cleared the tea cups and wrapped the tea loaf.

She left Nona sitting there, grabbed her quilt from the kitchen, and headed upstairs to her room. She laid the quilt out over the bed. The tea had done its job—for her, at least—as she was sufficiently calm now. She changed in the small en suite bathroom. In bed, she curled up in her princess quilt, but she couldn't escape the blasted stain. She wrote herself a reminder, "Stain Maid—Quilt Shop," on the little notepad on the bedside table.

7

DÉJÀ VU

ALEX ASSUMED SHE WOULD HAVE SLEPT AS SOUNDLY AS SHE had the night before because the neighborhood was so quiet. There were no city sounds of screaming fire trucks, honking horns, or lively party-goers. Instead, the sheer quiet, with only the ambient sounds of the night, kept her awake. She heard the drumming vibrations of the cicadas at dusk. It was the pulsating call of the katydids and the chorus of the frogs that had kept her awake.

Alex stirred in her soft down surroundings. She could feel the exhaustion in her eyes. What little sleep she had gotten had been filled with bizarre dreams of growing stains taking over whole quilts. She truly hadn't had a minute to settle since arriving on Spruce Street, and without much sleep, she was feeling pretty cranky. She grumbled about not being in any mood for Nona's nonsense today while brushing her teeth.

Downstairs, she found the house empty again, at just after nine a.m. Alex decided to indulge in another of those delicious hot chocolates from the Rise and Grind Café and maybe splurge on a croissant.

She headed over to the café. Joey, the young man from

yesterday, greeted her with a smile. He had a pleasant greeting for Alex and got right to taking her order. "What can I get for you this morning?"

"Small hot chocolate with no whipped cream," Alex ordered.

"No need for the extra calories," Joey replied back.

Smart kid. Alex grinned before replying, "That's right! I think I will put those calories into a chocolate croissant today. Do you live around here, Joey?" Alex questioned, making small talk, trying to blend in with her new non-lawyer crowd.

"No, I live on the southside of town," Joey replied. "My new grandmother is sending me to the community college, so it's more convenient to work in this area."

Joey conversed with Alex naturally, the way a good barista would. She hadn't missed what he'd said, though. Was it strange that she picked up on "new grandmother"?

"Besides, my neighborhood is too gossipy," he replied with a straight face before turning to make the hot chocolate.

And right on cue, as if the gossip gods had summoned her, Alex heard that familiar squeaky voice behind her. "Hi, Alex," Betty said in a singsong voice.

"Hi, Betty," Alex replied, turning and greeting her with a fixed smile.

"Good morning. It's going to be a busy day today," Betty stated matter-of-factly, as Joey handed Alex the hot chocolate and croissant. "You and Nona are going to change the will today? To cut Jack and Charlotte out of it?" She posed this as a question, but Alex knew Betty didn't expect an answer.

Alex ushered Betty toward the table and away from the prying ears of the customers in line behind them.

What on earth? It's only nine-thirty in the morning. How does she know? Nona!

"Nona and I got to chatting, you know, while we were in

line at the Pop and Shop this morning. Will you be at the quilting meeting tomorrow?" Betty said in one breath.

The woman can finish whole paragraphs before coming up for air.

"Yes, I will," Alex responded.

"Well, it makes sense, it being your house and all," she said and shrugged.

"Well, I will see you at the meeting, Betty," said Alex while turning to leave.

"I'm bringing a special strawberry chiffon pie," Betty's voice trailed off as Alex left the café.

Alex loved strawberries and just thinking about the chiffon pie had her mouth watering all the way to the car.

In her rental car, she found herself staring across the street at the quilt store. It was a luxury being able to shop for quilting supplies right here in town, especially since there wasn't anything close to Alex in the city. She could surely use some more retail therapy. *Oh, and the Stain Maid too.*

The gentle chime of the door announced her entrance into the shop. It always made her happy to be here. She was surrounded by rich bold colors, as bright as the eye could handle. She just couldn't resist smiling. Sue was a master at bright and cheery, from the displays with fun little projects to the fabric on the shelves and the quilts on the walls. The shop matched her personality.

Sue came out from the back as Alex began to fondle some new batiks. She hadn't seen these yesterday when she'd come in, but she hadn't really looked around much.

"Hey there, Alex," Sue greeted her with a bright smile. She had on a chartreuse polo shirt and black pants that only served to make the chartreuse that much more *chartreusey*. "It's like *déjà vu*. First Nona and now you. Just like yesterday," Sue teased.

"Yes, I feel like I am in a loop from *Groundhog Day*. So, Nona was here this morning?"

"Yes, she picked out some fat quarters to give to the ladies at her quilt meeting. Are you going to be there?"

"Yes, of course. It is my house, after all," she said, mocking her previous conversation with gossipy Betty.

"Oh, that's great! I was going to swing by with my dish after I closed the shop, but I gave it to Nona when she came by earlier. All you'll have to do is warm it in the oven for about 20 minutes at 375 degrees."

"I'm sure she'll have Pam take care of it. Oh, before I forget, do you have any Stain Maid?" Alex asked with a hint of a frown.

"Sure do. The Grandmother's Secret Stain Remover didn't work?"

"No." Alex shrugged.

"Those are some gorgeous ombre batiks," Sue noted, nodding in Alex's direction, and Alex realized she was still petting them. "I just put them out this morning."

"Good," Alex said unconsciously, giving them one last pet. She didn't know what had gotten into her. *Nona, that's what.* "I will take two yards of each one for my stash," Alex blurted out.

"Perfect." Sue began bringing the six bolts to the cutting counter. "I hear you are going to be busy today," Sue said and winked at Alex.

"Nona!"

"I understand." Sue laughed. She was having fun with it, not prying and expecting information like Betty did.

Alex really enjoyed Sue's company. Sue was older but closer in age to Alex and Charlotte versus Nona and Betty. Even though she seemed to be in the center of a lot of neighborhood gossip, she wasn't gossipy like the others.

"Nona also demanded I bring my gran's iced tea. All this must be in honor of you being home?"

Alex shrugged, mesmerized by the rich cascade of colors in the ombre fabrics Sue was cutting for her.

"She doesn't usually make this much of a fuss over us at the weekly meetings," Sue said as she was ringing up Alex's purchase. Alex was going to have to buy some new storage containers if she kept up this routine.

"Ha, you're right," Alex said. Her curiosity was piqued. *What is Nona up to now?*

"I will see you tomorrow," Sue said, winking and giving Alex a grin that would make the devil squirm.

Alex left the shop with her fabric, feeling lighter even though she was twelve yards heavier now. She was *much* better in fact and ready to deal with Nona, the will situation, and the craziness going on at number 1.

Alex was assuming she would be able to talk Nona out of cutting Charlotte out of the will at least. Jack was another matter. She figured Nona was going to dig her heels in. She would give the town clerk, Lucy, a call to notarize the paperwork once she had drawn up a will to execute Nona's wishes.

As she pulled up in front of her new, old home, she steeled herself for an epic battle with a formidable opponent. The thought made her sigh. She hadn't gotten this worked up over the unsavory clients she'd dealt with at her law firm.

Thinking of her law firm, she realized she hadn't heard a peep from the big city in two days and had almost forgotten what she had left behind. The transition of her clients had been too smooth. She had been expecting a tidal wave of backlash from the firm and family, but it had all been too easy. She didn't mind, but the last meeting she had with the two partners hadn't sat well with her. There was an unsettling feeling that she wasn't getting away that easily.

8

DOWN TO BUSINESS

Pam motioned to Alex that Nona was in her bedroom. "I wouldn't go in there if I were you."

"What's going on now?" Alex asked as she removed the cover from her now cold hot chocolate. She got a small plate from the dish strainer, which she used for the croissant, and put both croissant and drink in the microwave together to heat up again.

"Jennifer was here," Pam said, as Alex removed her breakfast from the microwave.

"Seriously?" was all Alex managed to say before biting into the croissant and burning her tongue. "Ouch."

Pam bobbed her head. "Yes, quite serious."

Alex could see the irritation as Pam scowled. Alex realized Pam had been dealing with Nona's nonsense for two weeks now, ever since Jennifer had come to Spruce Street.

"I just don't know what has gotten into Nona recently. I've been away the last few weekends, but surely, she can handle herself for those two days of the week? She has been acting so—"

"—like a teenager," Alex finished her sentence, and they

both chuckled. "I am going to catch up on this month's book club book while we await her royal highness."

Alex gave a mocked bow in the direction of Nona's bedroom door, and Pam playfully swatted a towel at her.

Alex curled up on the overstuffed loveseat with her eReader and one of the spare quilts hanging over the back of the loveseat. Alex appreciated the bright colors in the spare quilts that distracted her eye from the hideous loveseat.

She read and drank her hot chocolate as the midday sun beamed in through the large picture window warming the side of her face. She was so peaceful that she fell asleep. When she woke, Nona was standing over her with her hands on her hips staring down at her.

"Did you enjoy your siesta?" she teased. "Let's get to business."

Alex could see Pam standing in the entryway. "I'll let you get to business then," she said and gave Alex a good luck smile. "I have to make cookies for the meeting."

Nona pointed to Alex's shirt sleeve. "You know, you were snoring, and drooling."

"Yeah, yeah." She wiped her cheek. She hadn't had a moment's peace since she'd arrived, and the lack of sleep had caught up with her. "All right, Nona. Why have you been going around stirring up the gossip mill again?"

"I've been doing no such thing," Nona retorted. Her forehead wrinkled, and her lips pressed in a firm white line.

"Okay, fine! Have it your way. Have you given any more thought to what you want to do about Charlotte? Your argument that she is too modern is without merit."

"Yes, I suppose I was overreacting about wanting to cut her out," she conceded. "Just put in something suitable for her. I will leave it to you." Nona patted Alex's hand.

Alex was beginning to feel like she was a character in *Alice in Wonderland*.

"I can do that. What about Jack?"

"No, no, no. That floozie won't get a dime. Did you know she can't even cook?" Nona asked with a disgusted expression. "Who marries a woman who can't cook? I tried to accept her several times," Nona said flippantly. "I ate her tea loaf. It was okay. Not as good as Betty's. I even extended the olive branch by letting her pick out fabric from the closet. For Jack's sake, of course," she spurted, "but I just know she's bad news. Let's see what happens when the spotlight is on her at the quilting meeting."

"You mean you extended the 'fabric stash'?" Alex joked, adding air quotes to *fabric stash*, otherwise known as Nona's fabric closet. "I told you the tea loaf was good, but you didn't believe me." Alex winked. "I hope you left me some."

She wasn't sure what Nona had up her sleeve for the meeting. It might be like chumming shark-infested waters. Alex shuddered at the thought.

"She picked the ugliest piece of fabric in the closet. As soon as she left, I called over there to remind Jack to make sure that bimbo brought something to eat for the quilt meeting."

"Nona, please tell me you did not call her a bimbo to Jack? She's his wife! If you are not careful, he might have you committed."

"No, of course I didn't say that to Jack, but you started all this."

"Wait," Alex interrupted. "I didn't start all this." She was reduced to sounding like a teenager herself.

"Never mind that." Nona dismissed her with a wave of her hand. "Jack said he had the day off, and he would bake something nice for the ladies. My own son, reduced to baking on his wife's behalf. This woman has him wrapped." She held up her two fingers wrapped around each other. "He's in *love*. He isn't thinking with his brain."

Alex took a minute to collect her thoughts. "I am not sure how to respond to all this, Nona. You really need to stop calling her names. It is childish. Her name is Jennifer."

"Jennifer, Jennifer, Jennifer," Nona went on saying in a singsong voice. "Yennifer who can't cook."

"So childish, Nona," Alex shook her head. "Are you in the right frame of mind to be drawing up legal documents? Or should I call Doc over for a house call?"

Nona made the hand gesture of zipping her lips like a schoolgirl.

Alex hated to play the doctor card with Nona, but she knew it would get her back on point. Nona was known for her no-nonsense demeanor, but she was terrified of being found incompetent, and the thought of being sent to an old age home scared her senseless.

"Secondly, it seems like Jack is just trying to be nice to his new wife and help her fit into the group. You ladies aren't the most inclusive bunch," Alex scolded.

Nona made an incoherent noise of protest and dismissed the comment with another wave of her hand.

Alex said, "Look, I will make sure there is something generous for both Jack and Charlotte and enough for you to remain comfortable." When Nona began to argue back, Alex stopped her, saying, "Hear me out. I will put a clause in that, in the event something happens to Jack, his portion will revert back to Charlotte. Happy?"

"Fine."

Alex continued, dismissing Nona's scowl, "I will draw up the paperwork this afternoon. In the meantime, stop gossiping about money and wills."

"You are my best girl. You know that, right, Alex?"

"Yes, I love you too," she replied with a gentle hug.

She couldn't understand why Nona was going on the way she was to begin with, but it would soon be all settled for Nona's peace of mind.

Nona had access to an account that had nearly a million dollars in it, but that was just a fraction of Alex's wealth. There was no way Jack or anyone besides Alex would have access to it if something happened to Nona. Alex had made sure of it. It was her money after all. With the way Nona was acting, it seemed a good time as any to get everything resolved. At Nona's age, it didn't make sense for her to have the unnecessary pressures.

Alex spent the afternoon drafting the documents. She started with a living will, then the legal documents to remove Nona from the ANB Inc. account, and finally a simple will in the event of her death. It was morbid to think about because she was so close to Nona, but she tried to think of it like one of her cases. She was a skilled defense attorney, but she had done plenty of estate cases over the years, working pro bono for a small charity in the city.

After all the paperwork was in order, Alex logged into the online banking system and began the transfer request through the bank. She moved the bulk of the money left in the joint account back into her own personal account. She was surprised at how much money Nona had used but not surprised really given all the things she'd accomplished. All the things Alex knew about, that was.

She left plenty for Nona's living expenses, her daily salon visits, and regular trips to the Nuts & Bolts Quilt Shop, of course. Now that Alex was home, she could handle the few household bills and pay them straight from her own bank account.

She put the agreed amount Nona wanted to leave Jack and

Charlotte in the savings account attached to the checking account. Nona would still have access to that as well, if she needed it.

She brought the forms down for Nona to review and sign, which Nona did begrudgingly. Pam served as a witness. She really should've had two witnesses, but it wasn't a complex matter, and there really wasn't anything for anyone to contest. Pam didn't read the documents. She simply asked Nona if it was what she wanted, and Nona confirmed with a nod, and Pam signed.

After a stressful day, Alex spent the rest of the evening unpacking more boxes she had stacked in the spare room, mostly clothes and things she needed right away and mementos and important items that she hadn't wanted to pack in the POD, just in case anything had happened in transit from the city.

By the end, she was exhausted and decided to clean her quilt and try to wash her feelings away. She brought her quilt into the bathroom with the Stain Maid. The directions read: *Run the crayon over the stain, creating a thick layer. Gently agitate the stain. Dab with clean water or rinse.* Alex followed the instructions to no avail. She left the quilt hanging on the towel rack to dry.

This stain wasn't budging. It was turning out to be more stubborn than most of the prosecutors that she'd faced!

9

THE QUILTING MEETING

THE NEXT MORNING, ALEX HEARD THE FRONT DOOR opening and closing. She hadn't realized the time. It was already time to head down for the quilt meeting and brunch. No doubt Nona would make a fuss over her *"best girl"* being home. Alex had hoped that the fuss was going to be for Pam instead. It was nice for everyone to get together to say goodbye to Pam. And there was Jennifer. She would be coming as well.

Downstairs, the hum of friendship and laughter filled the air. Alex greeted a few of the ladies with warm smiles and gentle hugs and accepted their cereal box contributions.

One of her chosen tools, Nona used the cardboard cereal boxes for her quilting templates, mostly cut into hexagon shapes for her Grandmother's Flower Garden quilts. Since cereal boxes were one of the approved quilting tools on Nona's list, everyone on Spruce Street saved their cereal boxes like their lives depended on it. Even twenty-five years and four hundred miles later, Alex had struggled to put them in her recycle bin.

Alex could see through the doorway that there was quite a spread of food on the dining room table already. She was famished and couldn't wait to dig in.

The doorbell rang, and everyone quieted. Alex gave the women a formidable stare before opening the door to find Jennifer holding a casserole dish.

"Hi, Jennifer. I'm so glad you could join us," Alex greeted and reached for the dish. "Here, let me take that so I can introduce you to everyone, and we'll put this—"

"It's a lasagna," Jennifer interrupted. "I made it myself."

Alex wondered if Jennifer had made it or if Jack had.

"Sure, she did," Alex heard Nona say.

Alex turned in Nona's direction and gave her a wide-eyed stare. Translation, *You'd better be on your best behavior.*

"Thank you for the invitation. It was kind of you and Nona to welcome me into the group," Jennifer said.

Alex made introductions as they made their way toward the dining room. She caught sight of the special floral fabric peeking out of Jennifer's bag. Most of the women were nice enough to at least nod when Alex introduced Jennifer, but the cold shoulder was clear. By their lack of interest, which was just plain rude, it was clear none of them were going to accept Jennifer into the fold. She was closer to Charlotte and Alex's age, so Jennifer would be more comfortable at the guild meetings at Nuts & Bolts. Alex couldn't believe Nona was acting like this again.

Alex showed Jennifer to a seat where they could sit together. It was important to make her feel welcome even if Nona was going to throw her to the wolves. Jennifer had done nothing to Alex, and Nona hadn't made a convincing argument why she was no good. Alex still believed in the Eleventh Amendment—*innocent until proven guilty.*

Nona gave a reminder for next month's book club meeting date and the next book, *Death Aboard the Meander—A Quilting Cruise Cozy Mystery.* They passed around the basket of fat quarters that she'd bought at the quilt shop. The women pawed through all the pretty fabrics, each selecting their favorite to take home as a gift. Nona then moved on to show-and-tell. Each of the women had brought at least one item they had been working on or finished. They went around the room taking turns. "Oohs" and "aahs" sounded all around.

One bohemian-looking woman with spiky purpleish hair showed the group a stack of sixty degree table runners.

Alex could never remember her name. *Kathleen? Katlyn? Karen? She's been busy.*

"Overachiever," Jennifer mumbled, and Alex laughed.

"Wait until you see what Nona shows," Alex whispered back.

A few women were working on panel quilts for the group's charity efforts. Another woman was busy hand-stitching the binding on her Quilt-As-You-Go Christmas tree skirt.

When it came around to Nona's turn, she went into a five-minute rant about her favorite quilts, the only ones she ever made, Grandmother's Flower Garden quilts. "English paper piecing, EPP for short. My quilts were all made from small one-inch or two-inch hexagons." She showed the ladies a pile of small hexagons, each about the size of a quarter. "The centers are often yellow, surrounded by a round of six solid hexagons and then surrounded by another round of twelve much prettier fabrics. These 'flowers' are stitched in rows with green between them. The green represents the grass, or it might be white hexagons representing a white picket fence."

The women feigned interest because, of course, they already knew all this. This show was just for Jennifer.

"Historically flour sack prints would've been used. They often made the hexagon shapes with newspaper or other light cardboard templates. In my case, those cereal boxes you all have been collecting for me!" She showed a small table topper as an example and then the quilt from the couch. Nona finished her show by pushing the quilt toward Jennifer. "As you can see, the edges were whip stitched closed, by hand, in what is commonly called a knife's edge technique."

Jennifer didn't seem too impressed. It was possible she just wasn't into quilting.

"I don't know how I am going to follow that," Pam conceded before showing off a gorgeous stack-and-whack quilt top she was working on for her mom. She had made it with some of the floral fabric from Nona's special stash closet.

After her spiel, Alex was watching Nona guzzle her glass of water and blot her face with a hankie. Then, Nona frowned at the woman beside her and whispered something Alex couldn't hear.

Alex saw Jennifer start to relax. It seemed like she was trying, even if she was not so interested in quilting.

Nona must have seen it too. "Why don't you show us the fabric you chose?" Nona asked her, akin to a bloodhound trying to catch its prey.

Jennifer sighed, and Alex watched her tense up at being the center of attention. As Jennifer stood, Nona excused herself to go to the bathroom.

"That was rude," Alex whispered.

Pam, who was sitting to the right of Alex, said, "I'll go check on her in a few minutes."

Alex gave Jennifer an encouraging nudge to show her fabric.

"I chose this cactus flower print. The white flowers remind me of the state flower from my home state of Arizona, where I grew up."

"Oh, that's nice, dear," Alex heard from one lady across the room as she stood up and began showing her quilted potholders.

Jennifer sank into her empty chair, her cheek twitching in irritation.

"Don't pay them any mind." Alex chuckled, holding out her

hand for the fabric. Nona wasn't kidding when she said that Jennifer had picked the ugliest fabric in the closet.

A few more ladies showed projects they were working on, and Betty announced her upcoming pie of the month, pecan pie. "Time to order, ladies," she said and handed out order forms.

Since Nona was still in the bathroom, Betty spilled the beans to everyone about Pam leaving and Alex being here to stay for good. With the attention focused on Pam, all the women huddled around her, and Alex got up to get a plate of food. She was feeling peckish. Her stomach had been poking her to eat throughout the whole meeting.

Sue's gran's special iced tea was especially satisfying in the chilled glasses that Pam had put out.

"Yum," she murmured as she sipped the sweet tea. Everyone was too busy inspecting each other's projects and talking to Pam to notice Alex hovering over the food.

The lasagna had been cut into, one piece removed, though it looked as if Alex was the first through the makeshift buffet. She was salivating with anticipation. She had missed all this home cooking over the years.

Just as Alex was about to settle into her plate, Pam let out an ear-splitting shriek from behind her. Alex jumped out of her seat. Tea and lasagna went flying everywhere.

Pam was in Nona's room just behind Alex. The bathroom door was wide open, and Pam was shaking Nona, who was sitting on the closed lid of her throne, slumped over the sink, with two unstitched hexies in her left hand. The fingers on her right hand were blue, and her hand was outstretched. It was as if she was trying to reach for something and had dropped her needle and thread in the sink.

"Call Doc!" Pam yelled.

Alex went to Nona. Her lips were blue too. "Nona," Alex

beckoned, pushing Pam aside and giving her a shake just as Pam had been doing when Alex had entered. Even though she already knew Nona was dead, Alex checked for a pulse to be sure.

"She's dead," she whispered into the air.

10

THAT HAPPENED FAST

Doc was the first to arrive just minutes later. He was already on Spruce Street, making a house call to Pete at number 11 who had cut himself trying to sharpen his lawn mower blades.

"Ladies, please let me through." Doc cleared the human fence of women wrapped around the doorway. Moments later, he confirmed, "She's gone. I am sorry, Alex. She's gone."

Alex was calm for the moment. "Please do everything you can to find out what happened to her."

She was in shock but not the panicked frantic shock like the other ladies. The firm had trained Alex to stay her emotions in all manners of situations. As a criminal defense attorney, she had seen a lot of horrific pictures of dead people. That differed greatly from seeing Nona, lifeless.

The ladies stood murmuring and crying as the paramedics arrived and put Nona on a gurney. The paramedics covered her with a stiff white sheet. As they wheeled her out toward the front door, one lady grabbed the paramedic's arm and said, "Wait." She held up her hand.

They all stood there watching as she unfolded one of the

guest quilts from the back of the loveseat and gently laid it over her friend.

"I can't believe it," Betty sobbed.

"What happened?"

"Is this real?"

"Was it her heart?"

"Did you see her fingers?"

"She was fine minutes ago."

Alex heard the murmurings through the crowd of ladies, unsure how to process the unexpected turn of events and sudden death of their friend.

Doc gave Alex one last look, and she nodded back in response as he followed the paramedics out. The fire chief, Cole Cyrus, doubled as a paramedic when needed. He was also Jack's best friend. Nona had been like a second mother to Cole, and he called her ma, despite her protests to call her Nona.

"Jack?" Alex questioned as she realized someone needed to tell Jack what had happened.

"I'll take care of it," she heard Cole's booming voice volley back to her before the door closed.

Shocked but composed, Alex sat as she tried to console each of the ladies as they left one by one. She hadn't seen Jennifer leave.

When it was just her and Pam, they sobbed. Pam made tea, but Alex didn't touch her cup. Pam was always there. She was a member of their family. It was going to be difficult to see her go, especially now.

Caring for Nona perfectly suited Pam. Pam had come along five years ago. Alex had hired Pam as a nanny for the house and for Nona. Nannies for Nonnies was the service. Alex had thought it was an awesome name for a business. The company paired single younger live-ins with elderly singles and couples. Alex didn't tell Nona any of this, of course, just that she had found a nice roommate for Nona who was thirty years younger than Nona and could help her out around the house for room and board.

Alex had known from the start that Pam was suited to Nona. However, when Pam had first arrived, Nona thought had she was *a crazy witch*! While they appeared to be nothing alike physically—Pam was short and buxom with a long mane of wild curly red hair, and Nona was tall and leggy with perfectly coiffed hair—Nona had learned Pam was a no-nonsense woman like herself. Alex had slept well at night knowing that Nona was being cared for while she was so far away.

Now, Alex cried herself to sleep on the loveseat where she rested. When she awoke, she found Pam had propped a pillow under her head and covered her in a quilt. Alex pulled the quilt up to her neck, tucking herself into a cocoon.

The doorbell rang, and Alex didn't move. A second ring and she saw Pam pass by in the hallway. Alex heard the muffled sounds of a man at the door. To their surprise, floral arrangements, trays of cookies, and oversized fruit baskets arrived and kept arriving with increasing frequency. Every time Pam went to sit down, there would be another arrival. By dinner time, the living room was standing room only, and Alex had no choice but to get up to make room for it all.

Alex went up to her room to shower, change, and get her cell phone. She called Doc at the funeral home. He was the mortician as well as the coroner.

"What happened, Doc?" Alex asked when she got him on the phone.

After a long pause, Doc cleared his throat and stated, "I just finished checking the contents of her stomach. The only thing recognizable was pasta and chocolate." Doc hesitated for too long. "I sent it to the national lab, but the results will take a few days."

"Are you saying it was the food?"

Alex heard Doc let out a long breath and then say, "Well, her lips and fingers were blue."

"I noticed that too," Alex confirmed.

"I can only speculate it was something she ingested, an allergic reaction likely," he paused again before saying, "... anaphylaxis most likely."

"Okay, is that a natural cause of death or..." She left the "or" hanging in the air.

"Look, Alex, I checked her over thoroughly. There were no other internal or external physical signs that I could see, other than age, that would cause her death." Doc sighed. "She was in perfect health, otherwise, for someone her age." He hesitated and then continued, "Let's see what the pathology reports come back with, and then we'll know more. I don't want to cause a stir just yet."

"Thank you, Doc. It was just so unexpected and quick, one minute..." Alex trailed off.

"I know," he sympathized. "We'll keep her here for a few days while we wait for results. I'll have my secretary go over the arrangements with you and Jack, and I will call you as soon as I hear anything."

"Thank you, Doc." Alex hung up, uncomfortable with the unknown. She shivered at the thought that maybe it was something Nona had eaten or been allergic to or worse. *What about the other ladies? Did they eat anything? I surely would have heard from Betty by now if anyone got sick, right?*

Alex paced as she wrestled with her questions. She wasn't aware Nona was allergic to anything. *If it was food, it would have to be an accident. Jack made the lasagna. Doc said chocolate too. Jack wouldn't do anything to hurt his own mother. Don't get all excited over nothing. Stay calm and wait. Just wait till you hear from Doc. It's probably nothing nefarious. A decade of working as a lawyer has made my thoughts far too cynical.*

There wasn't much she could do without confirmation from Doc.

She could hear Pam downstairs and went down to tell her about her conversation with Doc. As she helped Pam throw away all the food from the brunch, she made a retching motion with her tongue at the thought of tainted food.

As she began to scrape the food into the trash can, she said, "We better not take any chances, Pam. I just can't believe all this!" Alex dropped the plate she was holding, and a dozen deviled eggs slid off onto the table and floor.

"You sit. Let me get that." Pam began picking up the eggs. "Slippery little devils."

11

A LIFETIME OF QUILTS

ALEX DIALED JACK AT HIS OFFICE TO DISCUSS NONA'S celebration of life.

"Hey, Alex, how are you doing?" he asked, his voice somber.

"I am hanging in there..." Alex paused for a moment. "I spoke to Doc, and he said Nona would need to remain with him at the morgue for a while longer ... but I think we should go ahead with the celebration of life ... sooner rather than later."

"Yes, yes, for the community and all her friends," he agreed.

"Pam and I are here to support you, with whatever you need us to do, Jack," Alex said, her voice cracking.

"You handle it, Alex. I'm confident that you'll do as she would've wanted."

Alex insisted she would support him, but he had also insisted that she and Pam handle the evening.

"I heard through the local gossip mill that you and Nona were working on a will. I'm glad you worked things out for her. You know, I had no interest in her business dealings with you, Alex."

"I know, Jack. There was never any doubt," Alex assured him. "Despite what the gossip mill had to say," she added.

"My mother was a very independent woman," he said with pride. "It was good that you both had each other. You were a gift to us, you know," Jack choked out, and Alex could hear him weep on the other end of the line as it disconnected.

Jack had always made a good living being mayor the last three terms, and he was looking at running unopposed again next year. His motto was "Wealthy in life." He didn't meddle in Nona's or Alex's financial affairs. He would've provided Nona with a good life had she not had Alex's money at her disposal.

Over the years, Alex had—both anonymously and with Nona's help—helped most of the neighborhood families, the rec center, the senior center, and many other worthy causes, including a few hair-brained projects too. With the joint bank account Alex had set up, Nona helped the neighborhood in any way that she had seen fit. It was the least Alex could do after Nona had taken her under her wing and picked up where her parents had left off. Less than a year after her parents' death, Alex had found herself living with Nona and having more money than any fifteen-year-old could spend over the course of a few lifetimes. Alex had received life insurance payouts from both her parents and an inheritance, which, when combined, was enough to keep all of Spruce Street afloat for a good while.

Alex didn't need to work at all, never mind in a career where she believed she was doing more harm than good. She had worked because Nona told her she had to. *You need a job. You need something to work at every day, Alex,* she remembered Nona saying on more than one occasion.

Alex and Nona had gone over all the plans for the financial accounts, and because there was no actual will, Alex had insisted they create one with all the customary details. It had been a struggle, and Nona's wishes had been sparse, but Alex had known what was expected of her. *Make it quick. Don't drag it on.* She had required Alex to promise to honor her wishes even though it was going to be in writing—a simple wake to celebrate her life and her quilts. *Nothing more. No expensive funeral. No theatrics,* Nona had said while pacing the dining room just days before. The whole thing had clearly rattled Nona.

Then, there was the stash. It was no surprise Nona had very specific instructions about how to deal with the fabric stash that was in her bedroom. She wanted her quilting friends and family to take any fabric they wanted from her treasure-filled fabric closet.

Nona also instructed Alex to bring out her quilts for her celebration of life. *You will know what to do with them,* she had said.

Alex hadn't pressed the matter. Sandwiched in the middle of all they had talked about, Alex had simply made a mental note to go back and discuss it with Nona at a later time. It was something easy that Alex thought she could handle right now. If Pam needed her, she would call out to her.

Alex went to the closet downstairs in Nona's room. It wasn't overflowing like Alex's closet had been. Nona had a curated stash of beautiful floral fabrics, and on special occasions, she would let a select few people into her bedroom and into her stash closet to choose a piece of fabric.

As she flicked through all the exotic florals, Alex noticed an EpiPen on the shelf above. It was looking more and more like there was an allergy that Doc was going to confirm. Since Alex was unaware of it, Nona had to have developed the allergy recently, and while it was a little strange for an EpiPen to be in the closet, Alex had found stranger things in stranger places.

Nona was just like most quilters who put their stuff everywhere. Alex had once found a needle and thread stuck into the toilet paper roll. This had been before Pam arrived. Alex had insisted Nona make up sewing kits for her needles, thread, and hexies. The biddies had fun with Nona about the kits. Each kit also included a unique pair of decorative embroidery scissors. The handles of the scissors included everything from storks to cats and unicorns to butterflies. Alex had even seen one pair shaped like a sheep. Nona had told Alex how the ladies had spent a few of their weekly meetings making up the kits for Pam's safety and sanity. Alex's eyes sparkled at the thought.

She heard a lawn mower out in the yard, and her eyes darted to the window. The shade was drawn, but it sounded like the window was open. *That's strange. Nona always kept the windows in her bedroom closed and locked.* She moved around the four-poster bed and closed the window. The landscapers came on a weekly schedule, so no one had to worry about maintaining the yard. It was a straightforward thing for Alex to have taken care of for Nona and the property.

She went back to the closet and maneuvered the stack of finished quilts off the shelf and onto the bed. Alex counted ten in total, all hand-pieced and quilted by Nona. She brought the pile of quilts out to the front porch where she could shake them and air them out a bit while trying to figure out what Nona meant by, *You will know what to do with them.*

Nona loved making hexies for her Grandmother's Flower Garden quilts. Everywhere she went, which wasn't very far, she had her hexies in tow.

Alex placed the stack of quilts on the porch swing. The top quilt was unfinished. There was a prepared binding, a label, and some odd hexies in a Ziploc bag tucked into the folds. The baggy slid off her lap. She hunched over to grab it off the deck of the porch.

"Ouch." She rubbed at her thigh where a stray sewing needle was poking into her. She couldn't help but smile. "Nona." She weaved the needle into one hexie. Taking out the label, she read it aloud, "Spruce Street—Gretta Galia."

At the sight of Nona's full name, Alex hugged the quilt tightly to her chest for a minute and set it down in her lap. Looking at it, you almost couldn't tell there was a traditional flower pattern. It was chaotic almost. She didn't understand because the images made little sense. In the center of one flower was a birdhouse, surrounded by bird fabrics. On another was a lawn mower surrounded by petals of unique grass patterns. She pulled up one of the other sides of the unfinished quilt. A pie surrounded by different fruits and baking items was in another. She inspected a couple more of the flowers and realized the pattern or lack thereof. The curious mix of hexies puzzled her. It was an eye spy quilt. *The pies and fruits, that must be Betty!* She placed her hand on top of it and made a promise to herself and Nona to spend more time with it later and to complete the quilt. From the looks of it, there were only a few flowers left to complete. She would just need to complete the outer round, and then she could attach them to the quilt top.

Alex entwined her fingers around the hexies in the bag, like they were coins, inspecting a few as she pulled them out. The curious mix of hexies puzzled her. She dropped them back in the Ziploc bag and sealed it tight. Alex folded the bag of finishings in with the quilt and started a second pile on the porch swing.

The remaining quilts all appeared to be completed. She assumed they went in order from most recent to oldest based on the fabrics used.

Alex stood to unfold the next quilt, turning it several times to find the label. The label read, "Funeral quilt," and was dated as completed this year. Alex stood there with tears streaming down her face shaking her head.

"Nona," she moaned out loud.

She had seen Nona working on this one the last time she'd

visited. It pained Alex that she'd never thought to ask Nona what she was doing with all her quilts.

Alex couldn't believe she had come home to care for her adoptive grandmother, and in just a few days, she was gone. She dropped beside the stack of quilts with her arm outstretched over the stack and rocked herself for a while.

These can't all be funeral quilts, can they? How on earth was she going to display them all?

Shaking open the next quilt, she found the label, and it read, "Joey Kingston." The date on the quilt was October of last year. *Could it be the barista from the café?* Alex questioned. As far as Alex knew, Nona didn't visit the café *ever*.

"I couldn't stop this from happening," Nona had said when they had put in the Rise and Grind Café across from the quilt shop. Alex had tried to assure her it was a good thing, but Nona wanted nothing to do with the change in scenery to her neighborhood.

Well, that was a surprise, Alex thought as she began folding the quilt back up. She could bring the quilt with her tomorrow and see if the young man's name was Joey Kingston.

Unfolding the next quilt more quickly, she was eager to find out what the next one would say, and she found the right corner with the label. This one read, "Henrietta."

"Henrietta who?" Alex questioned aloud. "No last name?"

She draped the quilt over the railing. It was a lap-size traditional Grandmother's Flower Garden quilt, though the colors were anything but traditional, in an array of teals and aquas, rich caramels, browns, and greens mixed with bright flower colors in the centers.

These all looked to be about one-inch hexagons. Alex made a quick calculation and estimated most of these contained over 4,500 hexagons each. She was sitting with a pile of ten quilts. The sheer magnitude of the work was staggering.

This bed-size quilt exuded a tropical sensation, like a tropical island garden. Alex plopped down on the porch swing again. She had known nothing about the purpose of these quilts, the amazing, dare she say, "modern," aesthetic to this otherwise traditional quilt pattern. Nona must have been working on them right under their noses. With such small hand-worked pieces, no one would have thought twice about a brown-, green-, or blue-colored hexagon, and the quilt was dated 2018.

What happened in 2018? Alex pondered. Nothing unusual that she could think of. *Pam was with us then. Maybe she would know.*

Nervous to uncover the next name, she began unfolding the fourth quilt down in the pile. The label read, "To my dearest Liam."

Alex sank into the porch swing. Her head was swimming with questions. *Had Nona been involved with a man? Another child no one knew about?* "Dearest," Alex moaned, holding the quilt tight to her chest. Again, no last name. It was Nona's handwriting and was dated 2015. The quilt pattern was just straight hexagons this time, no traditional Grandmother's Flower Garden pattern. The fabric choices were very masculine. She draped the quilt on the railing on the other side of the stairs.

Male? Lover or child? The questions resonated in Alex's head as she began unfolding the next one. She was well past confusion, and it piqued her curiosity.

This one read, "Rebecca Briggs 2012." *Well, at least this one has a last name.* A clue, something Alex could research. She draped it over the railing like she had done with the others.

The next in the pile read, "Alex 2010," the year she'd graduated from law school. The tears came, and she couldn't finish reading the tag. Alex fell into the lap of the swing with the quilt gripped tight within her hands and buried her face into it. She lingered, wrapped in Nona's gift. Nona had picked Alex up by the bootstraps when she had been wallowing in death's misery. Nona had guided her through high school, taught her the craft of quilting, had been her rock through law school, championed all of her achievements, and celebrated all of Alex's victories. Nona didn't always say it, but Alex always knew it. And here she idled with the ultimate example of Nona's unfailing love for her in her lap.

She wiped her eyes and began again. She read the quilt label aloud. "Alex 2010. You know you are my best girl. I love you, and I am so very proud of you."

Alex lost all composure. Nona had used her actions to *show* her love and pride with the quilt itself, and in her final writing, Nona had *said* it too. Anytime Alex would need it, all she had to do was read the label. It would be like Nona was speaking those very words to her.

Somehow, Nona had captured the spirit of graduation with this one. With dark jewel tones complemented by black and light gray, it was stunning.

The way she went on arguing with Charlotte over being too modern. *What a parody for a no-nonsense woman. Nona sure was complicated.* Overcome, she had forgotten there were a few more quilts.

The last three quilts in the pile were what you would expect. The labels read, "Charlotte," "Sally," and "Jack." Charlotte's quilt was a beautiful Grandmother's Flower Garden Quilt in soft pastels, a baby quilt, dated thirty years earlier. Charlotte was just a young girl when Nona had made this for her. Alex couldn't wait to give it to her. Charlotte was going to adore it.

The quilt for Jack's wife was the most traditional of all the quilts, perfectly appropriate for a daughter-in-law, and Jack's quilt was a hodgepodge of colors and fabrics. The label read, "To my son, Jack. I made this quilt from clothing and old quilts from generations of our family, including your father's old uniforms."

Alex was at the bottom of the pile. Her heart couldn't handle any more sentiment. She folded the unfinished quilt along with Jack's, Charlotte's, Sally's, and her own. Alex left the remaining quilts hanging on the porch. It would be a nice way for all to see the quilts when Nona's friends and loved ones visited for the wake tomorrow afternoon. She wasn't sure how she would figure out who the other quilts belonged to, but that was a mystery for another time.

She brought the funeral quilt in with her to display in the sitting room where they had set up a large framed photo of Nona. Alex paused and touched the glass covering Nona's picture.

12

A CELEBRATION OF LIFE

Jack and Jennifer were among the first to arrive the next afternoon.

"I'm grateful to you, Alex, for handling everything. Nona was always so proud of you. I am too," Jack said with outstretched arms. Jack gave her one of his famous bear hugs.

Alex's heart swelled, and her eyes tearful in response to his words and the display of affection.

"Have you heard from Doc again?" they asked each other at the same time. The manner of Nona's death wasn't far from either of their minds. "No," they both said at the same time.

Jack gestured to let Alex speak first.

"Doc said he would call in the next day or two," she said.

"Let's talk tomorrow in my office," Jack said and glanced sideways at his wife, who was indifferent to the entire conversation.

"Sure, I will come by in the afternoon after I go to the clerk's office."

Though Jennifer appeared uninterested in the conversation between Alex and Jack, there was an edge about her. Her posture was rigid, and her facial features were screaming with nervous tension. Jack put his hand on the small of her back almost as if he was prompting her to greet Alex.

"Alex," she said, and she leaned in for a patting hug.

"Thank you for coming, Jennifer." That was a foolish thing to say, Alex chided herself. Of course she would come. This was a wake for her new mother-in-law.

"I'm sorry," Jennifer replied, looking grief-stricken. She pulled a tissue out of her pocket and blotted her dry eyes. It seemed an odd response and reaction, but then again, Alex had just said, "Thank you for coming."

Alex led them back out onto the porch and explained the quilts. She gave Jack the quilt Nona had made for him.

"I don't know what to say, Alex," Jack said as he shook and sobbed.

"I know the feeling, Jack," Alex responded as he enveloped her in another bear hug. She didn't really see him as an uncle. He was nearly the same age as her dad, though he wasn't a fatherly figure in her life either. Hugging Jack reminded her how much she missed hugs from her own father.

They stood arm and arm admiring the quilt. "This is just beautiful, Alex, and to think she used old clothing she had been saving from our family. From my dad. And his uniforms from the military." Jack stood admiring the treasure, sobbing like she had never seen.

"She left quilts for all of us. It was heart-wrenching to go through them all."

"The quilts are nice," Jennifer interrupted. "I was looking forward to joining the group and learning to quilt too. Just before she..." Jennifer trailed off. "Well, Nona offered to teach me."

Now that was unexpected, Alex thought. Maybe she had gotten through to Nona after all.

Alex squeezed Jennifer's hand and said, "We were planning

on continuing the meetings here. You are welcome to join us, Jennifer."

When Charlotte arrived, Alex could see by the state of her hair, her puffy eyes, and smudged foundation that she was taking Nona's death hard, especially given the craziness of everything that had happened with Charlotte and Nona over the last few weeks, much of which no one understood.

"I'm just devastated that I was not at the meeting," Charlotte cried, mascara running down one of her cheeks. Alex handed her a handkerchief from her pocket. "Why?" Charlotte sobbed.

Like many others Alex had talked to, everyone wanted to know why and how. Alex had no actual answers yet, and she was trying to be patient with Doc.

"What happened, Alex?" Charlotte pleaded. The guilt in her eyes was haunting. Alex had to look away.

"I don't know," Alex replied, "One moment, Nona was standing there, the life of the group, showing off her quilts, trying to antagonize Jennifer too, and then a few minutes later, in the bathroom, with her hexies in her hand..." Alex couldn't finish.

Charlotte hugged her. "It must've been just awful for all the ladies," Charlotte cried, dabbing at her already destroyed makeup job. Charlotte went on to say, "I sent over a box of her favorite fudge. Even though she didn't want me at the meeting, I knew she wouldn't be able to resist the fudge."

That explained the chocolate Doc mentioned in his preliminary findings.

Alex tried to recall the memory of looking at the buffet of

food from the brunch, but she couldn't recall seeing a box of fudge on the table. It was likely Nona would have wanted to keep it to herself.

Her conversation with Doc echoed in her mind—two ingredients in her stomach, lasagna made by Jack or Jennifer and chocolate, Nona's favorite, specifically just for Nona.

Charlotte's face was bright red, and all traces of her foundation had vanished. Alex took her by the hand and brought her out to the front porch as she had done with Jack and explained to Charlotte about the stack of quilts.

When Alex handed her the quilt Nona had left for her, Charlotte's whole body gave way. She melted and fell onto the porch swing taking Alex down with her. Sitting on the swing, Charlotte held the quilt to her face and Alex could barely make out what she was saying. "Nona was so upset with me."

"I never figured out the real reason, Charlotte, but I do know she wasn't *really* upset with you." Alex shook her head when Charlotte let the quilt fall back into her own lap. "We had a productive talk yesterday, and she realized she was being foolish." Alex said.

Charlotte began to sob again, this time in relief.

Alex continued, "Honestly, I think she was just mad at Jack for marrying Jennifer, and you were an easy target, being you were so close. I understand your mom didn't want to be here at the same time as Jack and Jennifer, but there's a quilt here for her too. Nona loved her. She always said she was like the daughter she never had."

"Thank you, Alex. That helps a bit." Charlotte took a couple calming deep breaths and stood up to hug Alex with the quilt between them.

They both sat down again on the porch swing.

"I talked to Sue about you and me meeting at the quilt shop," said Alex, "but I think I should continue the quilt meetings here, for a while at least. Nona would want it that way, and we will welcome *everyone* who wants to attend. Not just *them*." Alex's joke lightened the mood enough to break the sad tension. "Of course I would still like to make sure we support Sue and the quilt shop."

"We can work on that together," Charlotte suggested.

"Yes, we will. We should transition the meetings over to Nuts & Bolts at some point."

"When the time is right." Charlotte finished her sentence like they had done when they were preteens, days gone by where they hung out in their bedrooms, dreaming of their husbands and making secret handshake promises to never lie to each other and to be best friends forever.

As Alex passed through the crowd of friends and family, she spotted the barista Joey tucked into a corner near the front door, looking as though he was teetering on making a run for it. This was a bizarre contrast to his friendly, assured demeanor in the café the last few mornings.

As she accepted condolences, she caught Joey's eye. He turned and made for his escape as she had expected. She followed him out onto the porch and called to him.

He turned to look her in the eye.

"Joey, I am glad you are here," Alex said.

Joey's look changed from panic to puzzled. "Me?" He pointed to his own chest. "Why are you glad *I'm* here?" He stressed the "I" in his question.

"Is your last name 'Kingston'?" Alex asked as he teetered on the last step as if unsure of what to do next.

"Yes, it is," Joey said, lowering his head.

"Nona left something for you," Alex said as she went to the porch railing where the quilt was hanging. Joey began climbing back up the steps. "Nona left these quilts, and this one is labeled 'Joey Kingston,'" she said over her shoulder.

"That's for me?" Joey stared up at her, open-mouthed.

"I believe so," she said as he climbed the final step back onto the porch.

"I don't know what to say," Joey began as if he couldn't hold back. "She already gave me so much." He wept and wiped his eyes with his sleeve.

"Come sit. Tell me about how you knew Nona," she said, resting her hand on the porch swing.

As soon as he was beside her on the swing, he began explaining that Nona had been funding his college tuition payments. "That's why I'm working at the café on this side of town. She said I was like the grandson she never had and that she wanted to keep me close." He laughed. "We met at..." he trailed off looking down at his feet, fidgeting with the quilt Alex had placed in his hands. "She barely knew me. I thought she was crazy for offering to pay for me to go to community college. I wasn't going to say no," he said, looking guilty.

Alex relaxed. "It's okay, Joey. There's nothing to feel guilty about. If Nona wanted to help you, that's amazing," she said with a friendly expression, trying to encourage him to open up more.

"It is much quicker to go back and forth to school and work if I don't have to walk all the way across town and back," he said matter-of-factly. "She was a good friend to me even though I am only twenty, and she was old, well, much older than me. I don't know how old she was, but she was more than just, you know." His youth was apparent in his eyes, pleading and desperate for her understanding.

"Yes, I know exactly what you mean, Joey," she assured him.

Even though he wasn't a client or in need of a lawyer, she felt like he needed her at this moment. Overwhelmed by her maternal instincts, she wanted to hug him. Unlike her clients in New York whom she couldn't hug, and even if she could, they were not the sort of people who were receptive to displays of affection.

Alex settled for a pat on his arm and assured him, "I will take care of you," and she meant it.

Alex knew she liked him from their interactions at the café. That he hadn't asked what would happen to his tuition payments now that Nona was dead spoke volumes of his character. She hadn't expected this, but it was just like Nona to find a nice young person to adopt into the family. After all, she had adopted Alex as her own, and Jack and Charlotte had welcomed her too. She had a moment of peace knowing she could help this young man in such a way that would honor Nona.

After a few minutes of awkward silence, they both said in unison, "She was a very generous lady." Then, they both sat back in a companionable silence until Pam came out looking for Alex.

"It's time for Jack to speak on behalf of his mother," she said in a soft voice.

Inside, Pam called everyone to attention, and Alex thanked everyone for the flowers, fruit baskets, and kind words. She planned on speaking to each of the guests later, and she let Jack have the room.

"Many of you have known my mother as Nona, and we have all joked that she got the nickname from being a no-nonsense lady," Jack began, and the crowd of friends and family murmured laughter and confirmations in response. "She was kind and giving, and she had a knack for judging good character. Nona was known to adopt people into our family." He winked at Alex, and he scanned the crowd as if he was looking for someone else.

Did Jack know about Joey? Alex wondered. Joey didn't say how they'd met, but she wondered if he was on Jack's radar. He didn't look like a bad kid. Alex was always good at reading young people. She had represented a lot of troubled youth in her early career as an up-and-coming lawyer in New York City. He seemed gentle and kind and was always polite. It only added to the unknown, so many questions and unknowns surrounding coming home to Spruce Street—Nona's behavior the last few days, skeletons in her closet, both good and bad, and also her death.

She sure was a complicated lady, Alex thought as she wondered what else was going to be uncovered in the coming days.

"My mother Gretta..." Jack continued.

After Jack brought them all to tears, Charlotte's love for Nona was on display. It was similar to how Alex felt about Nona but different. Nona had raised Alex because Alex needed her. Nona had done the selfless work of being Alex's caregiver because she wanted to, not because she had to. They, Alex and Charlotte, never had a rivalry about Alex being unofficially adopted into the family. Charlotte had always been independent, on her own path, and she seldom, if ever, got jealous of Alex's and Nona's relationship.

Alex was mesmerized watching Jack and Charlotte from across the room. Their resemblance to Nona was striking. Jack was tall and thick, with a strong back and broad shoulders. It made her wonder about his resemblance to his father. Nona kept his picture private. She had always said it was hard to look at too often. Jack's face was more delicate, though—the male version of Nona's with a long nose and broad chin. They were a formidable bunch. Charlotte could have been mistaken for Nona's twin from the family photos of Nona when she was Charlotte's age. The resemblance was incredible.

Alex wanted to talk to Joey some more, but she didn't find him again after Jack and Charlotte had both spoken. She saw Jennifer pacing around all evening. Alex had been to her fair share of funerals, but she couldn't recall seeing anyone behave this way. It wouldn't be easy, but she resolved herself to speak to Jack about Nona's concerns with Jennifer.

It was a lovely celebration of Nona's life. All the guests shared how they had known Nona, and many had comical stories to share with the crowd. They cried and laughed and cried and then laughed some more. Alex was inspired and filled with an abundance of gratitude for all her years with Nona.

Charlotte stayed to help Pam and Alex pick up. Together, the three of them made quick work of packing the leftover food into the fridge and cleaning up dishes. As was the tradition of the neighborhood, Pam would put the dishes out on the front porch and their owners, over the course of the next week, would pick them up at random as they had always done after every cookout, holiday, and gathering in the neighborhood. She couldn't remember when, but Pete had made oversized plate rails for many of the homes that had porches. It was quite the display to see the plates and platters all lined up after the parties.

Alex went to bed that night with a nagging feeling in her subconscious. She drifted into an exhaustive deep sleep and dreamt of visions of Joey sitting on the porch swing, Jennifer stuck to the corner of the room, Jack baking a lasagna and fudge squares, dancing across the dining room table.

"Doc!" she cried out in her dream before falling into a deep sleep.

13

THE STAIN

ALEX LOUNGED IN BED LONGER THAN NORMAL. SHE deserved an afternoon of hanging around in her sweats. Chewing on her lip, she was fighting the urge to follow up with Doc. He'd said he would call, and she knew how long these things took in a small town.

"Forever," she said out loud and got out of bed, yawning and stretching until she was on her feet. Alex caught sight of the stain on her quilt again. "Kiss-Off stain remover," she said and pointed at the stain, "that'll get you!"

Just an hour later, Alex stood outside the café with her cocoa in hand looking across the street at Nuts & Bolts Quilt Shop. This was becoming a habit, but there was no harm in it, and she needed to get the Kiss-Off anyway. Besides, she was rarely ever impulsive or irresponsible with her money.

She crossed the street and went in to pet some pretty fabrics. Forty minutes later, she left the shop with the Kiss-Off stain remover, a bag of Retro Clean Soak, and another dozen yards of gorgeous batiks.

Sue's words echoed in her ears. *Those just came in.* Alex

was wondering if she was being punked. She scanned the café parking lot just in case and laughed at herself for being so silly.

Sitting in her car, she remembered her big action item for the day was to call and check on the POD that was due to arrive tomorrow morning. Before she could fish the phone number from her purse, she heard a rapping on her window. She glanced up from her phone. Celia Moore was waving at her through her window. Startled, Alex put her hand over her heart, dropped the phone in her lap, and rolled the window down.

"I'm sorry. I didn't mean to surprise you, Alex."

Celia Moore doubled as the town's travel agent and real estate agent. Though she didn't live on Spruce Street, she was a friend of the neighborhood. She was an iconic woman, and Alex had always been envious. Her face was perfectly symmetrical, which made her stunningly beautiful. She always wore pointed toe stilettos with a pencil skirt that hung just past her knee and a fitted blazer atop a bright blue silk blouse. Alex had never seen her in anything else, even at cookouts and holidays gatherings.

"I was saddened to miss the celebration for Nona," Celia said with deep sadness in her eyes. "I was out of town when I heard from Betty that she had passed away, and I came back as soon as I could."

"It was a nice service," Alex said. "We laughed and cried. My face is still pink." She eyed her rearview mirror to check on the color palette of her eyes and cheeks.

"We all loved her. It is a sad time for the neighborhood," Celia said. "It was great that you turned it into an evening of celebration."

"That is what she wanted," Alex replied. "And far be it for me to do anything but exactly what she asked." A devilish smile crossed Alex's face, and Celia shook her head in confirmation that she understood.

"I am glad I ran into you, Alex," she said, smiling. "I have a package in my office for you from Nona. There's no hurry. Just come by when you have a chance."

Alex eyed Celia. "What kind of package? I am not sure I can handle anything more this week!" Her voice cracked.

"Just some paperwork. It's nothing for you to fret over." She patted Alex's arm through the window of the SUV. "It will be great to catch up. You can tell me all about big city life." Celia winked.

"I'd like that. My POD is arriving tomorrow, so I plan to spend some time getting settled in."

They discussed Alex stopping by later in the week. It seemed so contrary to her plans just days ago when she had thought of settling into her parents' house, Nona's house. No, now it was her house again. There wasn't anything else she needed to do in town, so Alex headed back to number 1 to tackle the stain and finish getting ready for the POD arrival.

With the quilt in her lap, she sat down on the lid of the toilet in her bathroom. Examining the package containing the little chap-stick looking container of Kiss-Off stain remover, she read the directions: *Dampen stain with water and rub in Kiss-Off. Alternate blotting with wet and dry cloths, until stain is gone.*

She tried for twenty minutes to get the pesky stain to release. She followed the directions, but it didn't work. Exasperated, she balled the quilt up and threw it in the shower stall.

She was frustrated and a little too hangry to do anything more. She took her phone off the charger on the dresser and called over to Jack's office, intending to leave a voicemail, letting him know she would come by tomorrow afternoon. The phone rang twice, and Frita, Jack's assistant, greeted her pleasantly.

Her POD was due to arrive at seven-thirty a.m., so they set a time in Jack's schedule to meet just after lunch.

Feeling extremely guilty about how she had treated the quilt in her frustration, she got the quilt out of the shower stall, unballed it, and then apologized to it.

One more try.

She brought the quilt and the bag of Retro Clean Soak to the basement. After reading the directions on the laundry soap, she filled the washing machine on hot and dissolved four table-spoons of the detergent in the hot water and immersed the quilt. She was confident that in forty-eight hours, the stain would be gone from her life and her quilt!

It was bittersweet that Alex was moving in and Pam was moving out. The two ladies had a light dinner together of deli sandwiches and potato salad. Pam had gone to the grocery store while Alex was out. Pam had filled the refrigerator and pantry with all the essentials, milk, bread, and cereal. Alex wouldn't have to worry about doing too much cooking. The fridge was already packed with containers and plates of food of every variety from Nona's celebration of life. She could live on all that food for at least a week, and Pam had frozen a good portion of the casseroles into single-serving containers.

"I hate to leave you here alone," Pam said. "Maybe I should stay another week until you get settled in."

"I will be fine, Pam," Alex assured her with a sly grin. "I have lived here a good many years, and I do know how to cook and look after myself." She winked.

"You sound just like Nona," Pam said with a heavy heart. "I have no doubts you can hold your own."

14

MEETING WITH THE MAYOR

Alex got up early the next day to greet the POD driver. They were a little late but arrived just before eight. She signed the necessary paperwork and went back inside to have breakfast with Pam and see her off later that morning.

Alex poured herself a bowl of her favorite Apple Snaps cereal.

"I am going to stay at least one more day," Pam insisted.

Alex turned to see Pam standing in the doorway, with her hands on her hips. Pam meant business. Alex had seen this stance before, and she knew, as had Nona, there was no changing Pam's mind.

After breakfast, Alex went down to the basement to check on the soaking quilt. She pulled up the corners until she found the one with the stain on it. *Dratz, still there! Twenty-four more hours, that's all you've got, you pesky stain. Be gone! As if that will work, but at this point, I'll try anything.*

She wasn't due to meet with Jack for a couple more hours still, so she busied herself unpacking the POD until it was time to head over to the town hall.

Town Hall Plaza was just three miles away. Alex gave herself a once-over in the rearview mirror and couldn't help looking back at the expanse of the now empty rental vehicle. It was a massive vehicle. In New York City, she had been accustomed to being on foot wherever she needed to go or getting Zoomer rides. She really had no need for a large vehicle. She resolved to head to the local dealership to turn in the rental and buy a car, something much more suitable to her new life on Spruce Street. She laughed at the thought. *My new life in Salem is what I mean.*

After a quick stop at the café to pick up coffees and a slice of Jack's favorite peanut butter pie, she arrived within fifteen minutes. The street was empty, so she parked right in front of the old stone building with the words, "Town Hall," carved stoically into a massive block of granite over the entrance.

Frita, Jack's assistant, greeted her at the reception desk. She was warm and had a motherly personality. She was very pretty for her age with her rich auburn curls that were shiny and bouncy. She didn't look a day over forty although Alex suspected she was in her early-sixties. For some reason, it made Alex feel old.

Alex handed the coffees to Frita. "These are for you and Jack. There is sugar and creamer there, if you wouldn't mind fixing it to his liking? And there is a slice of peanut butter pie too. Only if he has already had his lunch, of course."

Nona was one of those mothers who made her children, including Alex, eat everything on their plate but then rewarded them handsomely with a fine dessert.

"He has," Frita said, shaking her head and laughing. "He's waiting for you."

She tilted her head in the direction of Jack and headed down the opposite hall, toward the kitchen area. In the direction of Frita's nod was the hall that led to the mayoral suite. Alex could hear children yelling and hooting ahead of her.

The mayoral suite was an open area defined by a single desk for Frita just outside a door to Jack's office. There was one couch, a chair, and a coffee table on the opposite wall for people waiting their turn to speak to the mayor.

Now she could see the source of all the commotion. Jack was standing there with a room full of little kids. Many of whom were clinging to him. He was without his customary suit jacket and tie and had his arms curled out to his sides. Four little boys were hanging from him like a tree, two on each side. Alex couldn't help herself. She grinned with delight at the sight. Jack looked up, embarrassed to see Alex watching them play and began prying the children off of him.

"Don't stop on my account. That's impressive." This was what she had been longing for in the simplicity of her beloved hometown.

The children voiced their displeasure at having to stop playing with their new human jungle gym. Jack said, "All right, kids. Ms. Melo is going to take you back to school now."

Ms. Melo was the third-grade teacher at Salem Elementary School. She also used to live on Spruce Street in the family home now occupied by Alastor Arnold. Alex had had her as a teacher when she had been in school too. Her teacher had aged, but she looked just as Alex remembered her. Her face was free of any makeup, and she was neat and tidy with a skirt and sweater and sensible shoes.

Ms. Melo reached out, squeezed Alex's hand, and whispered her condolences.

"Thank you. It's great to see you again, Ms. Melo," Alex said.

"Ann, my name is Ann. You must call me by my first name now that you're all grown up, Alexandra."

"Please call me Alex, then, Ann," Alex said. "What a sight here, seeing our well-mannered, perfectly coiffed mayor acting as monkey bars for the kids."

"He's such a nice man, although I do apologize for keeping you from your meeting. Our Field Trip ran a little longer than expected." Ann pointed to Jack.

Alex could see it. Ms. Ann Melo still pined for Mr. Jack Galia after all these years. Poor lady couldn't catch a break when it came to catching Jack.

Ann corralled the school children into a line, and they all held hands as they left the building in a cute little walking parade, heading back to the school.

"I could've come back later?"

"Nonsense," Jack said, and Alex cringed at the word. It would always remind her of Nona. "The tour was over twenty minutes ago, but the kids baited me into playing with them." He laughed.

When Alex was within reaching distance, Jack pulled her in and wrapped her in a big bear hug. She almost melted right there on the spot.

Frita came up right behind them and chortled. She said, "Let the girl go, Jack. You'll smother her. She's a grown woman." Frita playfully swatted Jack on the shoulder with napkins. She gave him the coffee Alex had brought, and she set down the plated peanut butter pie. "Alex brought your favorite from Rise and Grind." Frita left with a wink to Alex.

Frita took good care of Jack. Like many good relationships, this one being strictly platonic of course. Jack knew who was boss, as did everyone else.

"How are you holding up?" Jack asked Alex.

She wasn't convinced with herself, but she confirmed,

"Good, I am good. How are you, Jack?" Alex asked, deflecting back to Jack, so she could regain her composure.

"It was sudden, and that's not easy, for anyone, at any age, but Jennifer has been a real support. She's a trooper. I mean, she's only been on Spruce Street for two weeks."

"It must be strange for her."

"She left everyone and everything familiar to her behind in Las Vegas to come here with me, and at her first quilt meeting, my mom...," he trailed off, shaking his head and steepling his fingers to his forehead.

"Yes, that must have been quite the shock to her. It was good of her to come to the quilt meeting, although Nona wasn't overly happy about it. The way she was going on about you and Jennifer," Alex said with a shake of her head.

Jack slapped his hand down on the desk, making Alex flinch. She was well-trained for such outbursts, but she wasn't on guard today. "It would've been better if she could've just been happy for us instead of going around town gossiping and ranting."

"Was there something else going on, Jack?" Alex questioned. "It wasn't like Nona to be so..." she trailed off, not wanting to say the word.

"Nonsensical?"

The way he said "nonsensical" made her cringe inside. She was desperately trying to hold herself together. It was different from being on a case when it came to your own family.

"Yes. Exactly. It was so out of character for her."

"The way Charlotte left and how she was taking it out on Charlotte too? She told me in no uncertain terms how she felt about Jennifer. I can't for the life of me figure out what got into her." He paused. "Jennifer has been wonderful. She gives me no cause for concern." He carried on, clearly looking to get this off his chest. "I mean, Mom even wanted me to do a background check on her." He didn't try to hide the shame in his face. Jack furrowed his eyebrows. "Of course, I asked Mark to do a quick search on her before I said, 'I do.' I *am* the mayor," he said proudly. "I have to be careful, more than just for appearances' sake, you know. Mark didn't find anything out of the ordinary. There was no valid reason for me to dig further into her past on the whim of my half-crazed mother."

Alex just shook her head. What was she to say, really? Though she did want to change the subject. Jack's face was turning crimson.

"Well, it seems Nona was a woman with a fair number of secrets. I wanted to ask you about the break-in. Did Officer Mark investigate? I found out about it from Betty. It didn't seem Nona was taking it very seriously."

"Mark didn't find anything there either. He chalked it up to general mischief and suggested we start locking our doors at night. Besides some minor property damage, it gave mother a fright and Betty something to gossip about, but that was all. You should be cautious, just in case."

"I will."

"There's been a lot of activity on Spruce Street lately." He listed off the highlights. "The son who no one has seen who moved into number 13, Jennifer and Kibbles, Charlotte moving out, you moving home, Nona's death, Pam leaving. The neighborhood hasn't been this busy in years."

She was deliberating his list. "True. Hey, one more thing, do you know Joey Kingston?"

"Sure, I know Joey. He's a good kid. Works at the café."

"Was he ever in any trouble that you know of?" Alex asked even though she couldn't imagine it, but you never knew these days.

"Yeah, Mark caught him and his friends at the park after dark. They're harmless kids. Sometimes 'Officer' Mark likes to razz the youth. You know, keep them on their toes and let 'em know who's boss." Jack guffawed.

"You are dating yourself with that language." Alex chuckled. "Did you mention that to Nona?"

"I don't see why that would've come up. Why?" Jack looked puzzled.

"I didn't want to get into it at the wake, but one of the quilts that I found in Nona's closet was for Joey. Of course I had already met him at the café, and my first impression of him was positive. Then, I saw him at the house and spoke with him about the quilt. He informed me Nona was funding his college tuition." Alex paused to see what Jack's reaction might be. He showed no sign of surprise, so she continued, "It didn't surprise me in the least, but I was curious how they would've met."

Jack sighed, remembering Nona's hard lost fight over the construction of the café. "She hated that café, even before it was built."

"I know," Alex said. "It just adds to the mystery that was your mother."

15

DOC

Frita interrupted and announced that Doc was on the phone looking for Jack.

"Put him through," Jack said. Into the phone, he said, "Doc, I have Alex here, and we have you on speaker phone."

"Oh, good. I was just about to call Alex too."

"Have you received the lab results back?" Alex asked Doc.

"Well, I have the preliminary results. They confirmed what I already knew, that Nona ate chocolate and lasagna in her last hours. Nonetheless, I am still suspicious that there is something else at play here."

Alex hid *her* suspicion that Jack might be a suspect. She still didn't know who had made the lasagna because it was a he-said-she-said situation. Jack said he would make it, but Jennifer said she *had* made it herself.

Alex was momentarily taken aback by the anger resonating from Jack's voice and his impatience with Doc.

"Be specific, Doc."

"We know her death was caused by an allergic reaction to something. For that reason, I'm still waiting on detailed results," Doc said.

Alex was having a hard time believing that something awful could happen on Spruce Street, or to her Nona, but she was growing uneasy, and so far, the suspects were people she considered members of her family.

"Well, she was recently diagnosed with a grass allergy."

"Yes, Jack. I let the lab know when I sent the sample, but I don't think it's that simple."

Alex knew this. She had seen the EpiPen in Nona's room, but with the events of the last few days, she hadn't the time or chance to ask anyone about it. Nona hadn't been in contact with grass, had she? That was such a peculiar question.

"She was *very* careful. There were EpiPens in the house if she needed them. She kept the windows shut," Jack insisted.

Has Nona done anything out of the ordinary this week? Not that she was aware of. Of course Alex had been just missing her all over town. Alex was one step behind Nona at the quilt shop two days in a row. Betty had said Nona had shopped at the Pop and Shop. She'd assumed Pam was with her. Alex was playing out the days leading up to Nona's death, only half-listening to the conversation between Jack and Doc.

"The window was open in her bedroom," Alex blurted as her mind flipped through the details. "I didn't think anything of it previously. I just closed the window," she said and shrugged. "I found an EpiPen in her closet when I was getting out the quilts. I didn't have the chance to question it. If there was an issue, why would the window be open? She would've kept it closed, especially knowing the landscapers came like clockwork every week on Fridays."

"Fridays," Jack said. "They're *supposed* to come on Fridays. She died on Wednesday, and you said you heard the landscapers on Thursday?"

"Yes, that's right. They were a day early."

"That's strange. Maybe it could've been her grass pollen

allergy. Sometimes, late-phase or delayed reactions can take up to twenty-four hours. Maybe in combination with..." Doc paused. Jack and Alex could hear papers being shuffled. "I'll update the lab, but I don't want to speculate any further. We will get to the bottom of this. Maybe Alex can do some digging on Spruce Street?"

"Yes," Alex said, still fully caught up in her own mind, going over the new details.

The grass pollen allergy explained all the trips to the beauty parlor, to have her hair washed daily, and the new wardrobe of handkerchiefs that Nona sported every day around said freshly washed hair. Nona was always out doing errands really early in the mornings.

None of this really mattered now though, did it? She recoiled as she felt the pain of loss resurfacing.

"Okay. Call me as soon as you know more, Doc," she heard Jack say as she saw him click off the speaker button and press "hold." He picked up the receiver and turned to his side to have a few private words with Doc.

After he hung up, they lingered in silence for a beat. Here was a man she had known nearly all of her life sitting across from her in complete control with his hands steepled, like the death of his mother was a business transaction, and Alex couldn't be sure *he* was not responsible for Nona's death.

"Jack," she said, "Nona told me you were going to make food, and when Jennifer arrived with the lasagna, she told me she had made it herself although Nona didn't believe her. You know, if this was an actual case—and it very well might still become one—you and Charlotte would be the main suspects here. Officer Mark is going to want to talk to everyone."

"Nonsense," Jack said and slapped the top of his desk again, making Alex flinch again. "This is a family matter. Our family," he added.

Alex winced at that word "our" again.

After a pause, Jack continued, "I did make the lasagna. I have nothing to hide here. Look, I know how this must look, but you know Charlotte and I would never harm Nona, right, Alex?"

"Of course," Alex replied.

Did she, though? She was beginning to question everything she knew about the residents of Spruce Street now. Was this going to turn out to be her hundredth case?

Did innocent people really say, "I have nothing to hide"? Countless times, she had defended guilty people who made "I am innocent" statements. She wasn't sure she could trust her instincts here. She was too close to it.

Jack took a deep breath and softened, saying, "I'm sure Jennifer only said that because of everything that was going on with Nona. I believe she was trying to fit in. She sincerely wanted Nona to like her."

Convinced that Jack was just too close to this, she left his office determined to do some investigative work while they waited for Doc to confirm. If Doc suspected foul play, he would surely report it to the authorities, and Officer Mark would get to the bottom of it. His father had been the one to break the news of her parents' death to Alex, and Mark had been a good friend to her. She'd crushed on him in high school though his eyes were only for Charlotte. Consequently, Charlotte never gave him the time of day.

Logically, it didn't make sense that Jack would do anything to the lasagna. He had no motive, and knowing that a room full of ladies would be eating it? But no one got the chance to eat the lasagna. After all, Alex had spilled her plate of food onto the floor upon hearing Pam's scream.

16

A PUZZLING TEXT

PULLING BACK ONTO SPRUCE STREET, SHE WAS REMINDED that the neighborhood was full of longtime familiar residents, many of whom Alex had known most of her life. Except for number 13, it was hard to think of all of them as anything but her extended family. The houses were numbered as they'd been built, so they were all out of order and numbered high to low as you traveled down the street.

Number 13, the first house on the street facing Main Street, looked to be occupied despite the fact that no one had seen John, who was Martha's and Roger's son. The retired couple were soaking up the sun and drinking margaritas in Florida, facts provided courtesy of the gossip mill, of course.

On one of their last phone calls, Alex had asked Nona about it, "Don't you think it's strange that no one on the street has seen John yet? I thought he was supposed to be renovating the house?"

"I went over there and scoped it out," Nona had replied. "Somebody is definitely living there."

"What does he do for work?" Alex had asked, thinking that might explain why no one had witnessed the man.

"How should I know?"

"Never mind," Alex had said, shaking her head at the phone. "How about you go and introduce yourself, rather than sneaking around? That would make more sense, don't you think?"

Nona had quietly murmured, "Unlucky number 13," over the phone.

Alex had suspected Nona had been making a sign to ward off evil.

Nona had continued, "It doesn't count."

"What doesn't count? Did I miss something?"

"It doesn't count. The house is technically part of Spruce Street, yes, but it faces the main road, so that doesn't really count ... obviously," Nona had clarified her statement for Alex.

"If you keep treating the property like an outsider, then it will continue to be one. It has a Spruce Street address, and the driveway is on Spruce Street. How does that *not* count?" Alex had asked.

"I never understood why they squeezed in two more houses. Couldn't they leave well enough alone?" she'd asked, not expecting Alex to answer. "Twenty years later, we could've bought up the extra land, and that would've shown them who they were dealing with."

Alex parked the car in front of her house and sat there quietly while pondering the facts and assumptions. Doc found lasagna in Nona's stomach contents, and there was already a piece missing when Alex had prepared her plate.

Charlotte had confirmed to Alex she sent fudge. *So the fudge was meant for just Nona.* But surely Charlotte wouldn't have told Alex that fact if she intended to harm Nona, and Nona could have shared the fudge with the group as well, potentially harming others. Finally, what was her motive?

Alex pulled out a pen and her notepad and began writing down the names of all the women who had attended the luncheon. She labeled the list "Attendees." She flipped the page over and began writing on the back side. She wrote Charlotte's name at the top, then she began listing out her thoughts, motives, and suspects.

Charlotte—not at brunch
Allergic reaction—food-related (Doc confirmed)

MOTIVES

Food
Lasagna—Jack (son) food for everyone
Fudge—(source?) Charlotte (granddaughter ostracized)
food for only Nona
Apple crumb—Betty (best friend)

As she was putting her thoughts to paper, she remembered Betty. Betty said that she and Nona were having apple crumb cake together in the mornings. This wasn't unusual, though. On Spruce Street, everyone ate pie or cake at any hour of the day, given the speed at which Betty pumped out the tasty treats. The residents of Spruce Street were accustomed to eating her delectables for breakfast, lunch, dinner, and dessert.

Will
Jack, Charlotte, Jennifer? (cut out of will)
Lucy? (town clerk/files all the paperwork)

Money
Jack
Jennifer? (daughter-in-law)
Charlotte?

UNKNOWN MOTIVES

Who had access to Nona?
Charlotte*
Landscapers—schedule all mixed-up
Jennifer—recently married the victim's son Money/un-
known additional motive
Pam—no known motive. (Nanny) leaving
Alex—no known motive (unofficial adopted daugh-
ter/granddaughter, recently moved back)
Betty—no known motive
Sue—no known motive
Ladies from the quilting group—no known motives

It was tragic to think of Nona as a murder victim. Alex went
back to her list and added everyone's relation to Nona. As she
filled in more and more details, it became clear that Jack, Charlotte, and Jennifer were still at the top of the list. *Were they all
in it together?*

She finished by making the list of all the places she knew
Nona had visited in the days leading up to her death.

Nuts & Bolts Quilt Shop
Pop and Shop grocery

A Better Cut—Hair Salon
Rise and Grind Café (?)
#1, #7, & #9 (?)
#13 (snooping)

She raged momentarily and crumbled up the paper. She threw the crumpled ball, and it popped off the steering wheel and came back at her, hitting her in the eye.

"Ow!" She couldn't help but laugh at herself.

She unfolded the paper in her lap and tried in vain to flatten it out again. As she stared at Charlotte's name, a thought struck her, and she added three more names to the list with question marks. The names on the quilts were most likely inconsequential to Nona's death, but she wrote them just the same as part of the facts.

Henrietta (?)
Liam (?)
Rebecca Briggs (?)

The phone in her lap vibrated with an incoming text. *Unknown number* was listed on the ID. She swiped up and typed in her password to see the complete message, which read:

Be careful, Alexandra. You are not free from the firm.
They will hit back.
I will do everything I can to protect you.

An involuntary moan escaped her lips, and she rubbed her temples trying to digest what she just read. *Be careful, Alexandra.* She only ever used her first name professionally in business, and, of course, when she was growing up, her parents had called her by her full name when they had been scolding her, like most parents did.

You are not free from the firm. With everything going on here on Spruce Street, she had all but forgotten to worry about the firm's reaction to her leaving.

Throughout her decade at Weitz & Romano, Alex had struggled with the clientele and often questioned if winning cases was actually really *winning*, especially in recent years with the higher profile cases, i.e., cases for the "family," as the firm liked to say. She questioned whether winning was more important than innocence. Her ambition to become a defense attorney had stemmed from her belief that she could truly help people.

She added the law firm to the list, though, surely, they would have taken action before she'd left the city.

They will hit back. What did that mean? Could this be someone from the firm trying to warn her?

Her brain whirled with questions. Who could the text be from? Would she be able to have it traced? Was it from someone inside the firm?

I will do everything I can to protect you. Who and how were they going to protect her? Alex's body began to tremble. Her calm exterior of the past few days was crumbling.

Alex typed, *Who is this?* and hit *send.*

She stared at the message screen. *Sending*—and then —*undeliverable.*

17

SAY WHAT?

A QUICK RAP ON THE WINDOW STARTLED HER. SHE ROLLED down her window, and the warm summer heat flooded her face.

"Hey, Alex. Sorry, I didn't mean to startle you." Officer Mark was standing there, hunched over slightly in line with the height of the window. He was dressed in his uniform, one hand on his holster.

"Mark, did you just send me a text?"

"No." His mouth said no, but his grimace told a different story. He was on guard, his eyes pinging back and forth unconsciously as he scanned his peripheral. "We need to talk," he nodded toward the house. "Inside."

"Yes, yes, of course." Her messenger bag was on the seat next to her. She took out her keys and grabbed the strap of the bag. Just as she was about to reach for the handle, Mark opened the door for her.

She used the ancient house key to unlock the door. Inside, she set her bag down on the loveseat, and Mark followed her from the parlor into the dining room where she offered him a seat at the long table. He pulled out one of the chairs and sat, bolt upright, and she knew he meant business.

Just because he was here on business, it wasn't going to stop her from being polite. "Would you like some spiced tea loaf?"

"No, thank you," he said.

"A drink? Some lemonade?"

He uncrossed his arms and agreed to the lemonade.

She reached up to the cabinet for two glasses. It was easy for Pam and Nona to reach the upper cabinets because they were taller than Alex, but at just five feet, two inches, without her heels on, she needed to stand on her tiptoes. She put the two glasses on a tray and retrieved the pitcher of lemonade from the refrigerator.

"What's going on, Mark?" She tried to be casual, but her questions always came out like an interrogation. "Is it about Nona? You have that look." The one she knew well from when they were teenagers. *The Look* that told her this was serious. Alex set the tray down on the dining room table and took the seat opposite Mark.

"Sorry, Alex. I'm here on official business, and it is very serious." As she poured the two glasses of lemonade, he surprised her by asking, "Have you talked to Doc?"

"Yes, earlier. I was in Jack's office when he called."

"Did he have anything new to shed light on Nona's death?"

"Doc said it might have been an allergic reaction to something she ate. I'm puzzled because I wasn't aware of it, but Jack said she had been diagnosed with a grass allergy. I can't imagine she would knowingly eat grass or that someone fed her grass, but the allergy would explain her new appearance with the handkerchiefs, the constant trips to the salon, and all the morning errands ... and keeping all the windows shut."

"Didn't even know that was a thing," he said and took a large gulp of lemonade. His cheeks puckered, and he tsked his tongue from the tart afterbite. Alex knew Pam liked to make the lemonade nice and tart. She flashed him a devilish school-girl grin.

"Until Jack mentioned it, I didn't either." She was still reserving her suspicions of the diagnosis. "I did a quick internet search, and it seems there can be more serious versions of hay fever ... but rare and not common to the extreme Nona was taking things," Alex said. "I was going to get some more information from Doc because she was acting so erratic." Alex topped Mark's lemonade. "Nona was rattled by something, and Jack getting married upset her as well."

He raised his hand over his glass to stop her pouring. "Of course, we've always known Nona wanted Jack to marry Ms. Melo."

Alex refilled her glass and sighed. "Neighborhood drama."

"It's more than that. Look, I'll be straight with you. We're investigating it as a case for murder."

"Neighborhood murder." She glowered. She suspected as much, but no one ever thought it would happen to someone they knew or in their own neighborhood.

"Why did you ask if I texted you? Earlier, when I first got here," he clarified.

She handed him the crumpled paper. "I was making this list in the car, and I received an obscure text." She pulled up the text and showed Mark the phone as well.

He read the text and set the phone down on the table. His eyes scanned the length of the sheet of paper, and then he flipped it over.

Unable to take the silence, she blurted out, "I want to help!"

"Well, that's the rub, Alex." He looked back at her and rubbed his temples. "We got a call from the FBI today. Nona's death was on their radar. That's why we're classifying it as a murder now."

"Why would the FBI be looking into Nona's death?"

"Well, they were pretty tight-lipped about the details, but what I do know is this…" Mark explained the call he'd received from the FBI, verbatim. "I can't believe I'm saying this, Alex, but it's a hit. Someone has put out a hit on you, and this bizarre text all but confirms it too. 'They will hit back,'" he quoted back from the text.

"Stop." She stood up. "You can't be serious. It's absurd." She stepped back and leaned against the wall.

"We have to look at everyone who was at the quilting meeting," Mark said, "and everyone not at the meeting too."

"Charlotte, Jack, who else? That's crazy." She waved her hand dismissing the notion. "It can't be her own family? Or one of the quilting ladies?" She shook her head. "Come on. No way."

She went to the fridge to get a bottle of wine and a wine glass hanging under the cabinet. She dusted the glass off and poured past the customary half-fill.

"I've seen a lot of crazy things over the years. This shouldn't surprise me." Alex sat back down at the dining room table with her glass of wine.

Mark's eyes were still scrolling up and down her list. "My money's on Charlotte. For Nona's murder."

"Why?"

"The fudge, your list, it was the only thing intended for Nona only." Mark pointed to the paper where Alex had made the note. "If it was something she ate?" He pursed his lips and cocked his head. "If it's not someone close to her, then it has to be connected to you."

"On paper, I agree it points to Charlotte, or Jack, but it's absurd. I'm not buying into that," Alex said, staring at Mark as she made the weak connection between Nona and the hit. "Connected? And what? Someone killed Nona"—her face contorted in realization—"to get at me?"

"Look, Alex, this is serious. What were you mixed up in, up there, in New York?"

She was mixed up in something all right. Corruption, yes. Power, definitely. But a hit? She was just a lawyer for a prestigious law firm. Sure, the firm possessed political control beyond what she was comfortable admitting, but she had always stayed on the right side of the law, not that she would voice as much to Mark.

"Well, there seems to be a lot we don't know here. Why's the FBI looking at Nona's death? Why was Nona ... murdered? Who took out a hit on you? And now, who sent you this text?" Mark questioned.

"And why?" Alex added.

"We're going to camp out here until we sort this out." He glanced toward the window, at his police car outside. "Officer Rigsby is on her way, and I'll be back tonight to see to your protection myself. In the meantime, call me if you need anything."

Mark was a stand-up guy, and he was highly respected within the local and state law enforcement. He was serious enough to camp out on her doorstep, but that didn't mean she wasn't going to try to figure out the answers.

He got up to leave and slid his chair under the tabletop. "By the way, do you know anyone by the name of Ray?"

She did. A client in New York with the last name Ray. Lucas Ray. She quickly explained to Mark how that case, the only case she'd ever lost with Weitz & Romano, unraveled with an unprecedented, last-minute change of judge.

At the front door, she raised a hand to wave to Rigsby, who was parked out front in her personal vehicle, an old multi-colored Honda. That was smart on Officer Mark's part and fast too!

She closed the door behind Officer Mark and locked the

deadbolt. The mechanism made a grinding noise from not having been used in a *very* long time. She checked the lock on the back door, which was hardly ever used, and, for good measure, checked all the windows too.

Two years prior—Alex had already won seventy cases when she met Lucas Ray. Not that she was counting at the time, but the law firm was, and the press was too. Her seventy-first case was a typical case. She was going before Judge Mackey, who was known for his leniency with Alex's clients. She suspected it was not because of anything she did or didn't do, but that unknown forces controlled the situation. The judgments were always in line with how the firm wanted the outcomes to be, but at the last minute, the case was assigned to Judge Sterne, whose name preceded him.

Lucas was just a scared twenty-five-year-old man-child caught in a smurfing and casino scheme—a white-collar crime with far-reaching consequences. What should have been a simple misdemeanor was trumped up to a felony, and suddenly, Lucas was national news and on the Feds' radar. They tried to use him as leverage to get the number one guy in their case. To Lucas's credit, he held strong and didn't give anything up, so they made an example out of him. Caught in a serious tug-of-war game between his loyalties to his employer and the FBI, he received an unprecedented maximum sentence.

This outcome was a disaster, and the partners were going to be furious, although nothing could have changed the outcome or the case reassignment.

Alex looked up and locked eyes with her boss, Remo Romano. She didn't like the look on his face. It was one of those "if looks could kill" moments. The thought of it made her tremble as she sank back into her seat.

In the brief moments Alex shared with Lucas before they took him off to prison, she saw his life flashing before her eyes. What do you say to a twenty-five-year-old kid? And what was she going to say to Remo? This was supposed to be a slam dunk. Lucas was in serious trouble. He wasn't built for crime or punishment. "I am sorry" was all she could say.

It was a hard loss. Alex fought hard to never lose again. She was filled with regret for this case despite convincing herself that she couldn't have done anything differently. Lucas's appeals would be handled by another lawyer, and as per the firm's policy, she would have no further contact with the client. However, for the last few years, guilt weighed heavily on Alex's shoulders.

Lucas was locked away, and everyone but Alex forgot about him.

Or so she thought.

EMAILS, NOTES, AND PHONE CALLS

To get her mind off the matter, she trudged down to the washing machine in the basement to check on the pesky stain. Tugging at all four corners, she didn't find the stain. Her eyes brightened as she rinsed the quilt and put it in the dryer. She rolled her shoulders and stretched her neck in relief. Confident the battle with the stain was won, she felt her spirit lift.

Inspiration struck. The source—Nona. If she could figure out what was going on with Nona, she could prove Mark and the FBI were wrong.

Alex stood at the door to Nona's bedroom. She didn't think anyone had entered the room since she'd pulled the quilts out. The door creaked as she opened it. She knew there was no one on the other side, but it was creepy.

"She's not here to see you go through her stuff," Alex told herself, though that didn't make it any easier. *I can do this! Nona would want me to.* Still unconvinced, she entered anyway.

The room was dim, and the air was stale from the windows and door being closed, but it smelled unmistakably like Nona. A bit of her freesia fragrance soap still lingered in the air.

She perched at Nona's desk in front of "the dinosaur."

Okay, it was actually a computer. It resembled the one Alex had owned when she was a teenager. Alex had wanted Nona to get a new one, but Nona had insisted this one worked just fine.

She felt around the back for a power switch and clicked it to life. As the dinosaur awoke, it emanated the familiar buzzing noise of computers of its age. Minutes later, the password screen was staring at her. Alex tried a few different names and dates, the obvious ones—Jack's, Charlotte's and her own birth dates. She even typed Betty's name although that seemed foolish after she typed it.

Too many unsuccessful attempts at the password got her locked out. She wasn't getting anywhere and still felt like she was invading Nona's privacy.

A thought came to her, sitting there in front of the dinosaur, the unfinished eye spy quilt. Maybe something on it would give her password inspiration. Plus, she was determined to get some work done on it.

Leaving the computer on, she rifled through the bills, odd papers, envelopes, and miscellaneous writing supplies on Nona's desk. She picked up a small sewing kit with needles and thread and a few finished hexagons. She scooped up the small stack of bills and headed for the door. The hexies filled her mind with a haunting vision of Nona in the bathroom, with the hexies in one hand and her other hand outstretched like she was trying to reach for something.

Alex crossed the room to the small en suite bathroom, flipped the light switch, and opened the medicine cabinet. The small mirrored cabinet contained three shelves filled with the expected items—aspirins, ointments, Band-Aids, a small sewing kit, and an EpiPen. *Was Nona reaching for the EpiPen? Was she aware of what was happening?*

Alex backed out and left everything else just as she'd found it. At the door, she bent to grab the trash can full of paper rubbish. She snuck out the door with the wire can as if she was about to be caught with something that didn't belong to her.

She dropped the pile of bills on the kitchen counter. The bills on top were unopened and postmarked the last couple days. Pam must've been putting them there. Alex sorted the stack of bills and separated out the junk mail. She ripped open the envelope for the telephone bill and scanned it for signs of anything unusual. Mostly local calls. As she rolled her finger down the list, she paused at an unknown number that appeared repeatedly. The bill catalogued the calls until the week before Nona's murder. She counted back the days from Nona's death on the large print desktop calendar. One call a day for eleven days prior to Nona's death, all at the same time each day, just after four p.m.

She dumped the papers from the trash can into the small blue recycle bin under the kitchen sink. One of Betty's monthly pie flyers caught her eye. It was on her trademark canary yellow paper, all crumpled up. It was strange because Nona usually kept Betty's flyers. *For posterity,* Nona used to say. She saved a pile of them in her stash closet.

Smoothing out the crumpled paper, she rubbed it back and forth against the edge of the table. It was this month's flyer for the flavor of the month, cherry pie. She laughed. She wouldn't have given it a further thought except when she held it up to read it, she could see something on the back. On the back of the flyer was a handwritten note, in all caps, that read:

YOU'RE GOING TO NEED YOUR LAWYER

Betty? Why would Betty write such a thing? When did Nona receive this note? Betty was Nona's best friend. Were they fight-

ing? Alex didn't see any indication that they'd had a falling out or anything had been amiss. *Was this some kind of gag or joke? Who would do this?*

All the questions were making her head hurt. Everyone in the neighborhood received Betty's flyers, so it could've been anyone, or this could be related to the hit. More questions blitzed her thoughts. *Why would Nona need a lawyer? Was this the reason Nona wanted to get me back to town? And if so, why didn't she just tell me what was going on? I was Nona's lawyer. Am I the lawyer the note was referring to?*

Darn it! She was ticked off at herself for not urging Nona to talk to her and downright mad at Nona for not just telling her what this was all about. As her thoughts and emotions rolled through her head, she landed on a suspicion. She was suspicious that this wasn't about Nona at all, but what was this all about? *Did it have anything to do with me? The firm? The family?*

Alex inspected the remaining trash—papers, flyers, scribble notes, to-do lists, and grocery lists. She carefully checked both sides of each piece. Only the usual papers you would expect to find and one side of a Sugar Oats cereal box, but Nona never threw away cereal boxes?

As she inspected the letter-size piece of cardboard, she found another note, written in the same capitalized lettering:

I AM COMING FOR YOU! —LVR

Who eats Sugar Oats? No wonder Nona was in a panic, Alex thought as she slumped into one of the dining room chairs. *Why hadn't she shown these notes to me?* Alex sat for a while with the small mesh trash can in her lap, gripping the papers.

More driven than ever now to find out who killed Nona, she

decided to enlist Hawk, the private investigator she'd been working with in New York. They had developed a closeness over the last few years. If she was honest with herself, she did have romantic feelings for him. She just wasn't sure she was ready to explore those feelings yet.

Although she no longer worked at the firm, she knew Hawk would do just about anything to help her out. She also sensed he might have deeper feelings for her as well though he'd never crossed the boundaries of professionalism or friendship. He would certainly be willing to help and could track the phone number at least. It was probably nothing, but she didn't have much to go on.

She gazed down at her phone. His number was so familiar to her. She'd dialed it so many times over the last few years.

Alex hadn't spoken to Hawk since she'd left New York, and he'd told her to call if she needed anything and to watch her back. It wasn't unusual that she would go a week or two without talking to him when there were no cases for him to assist her with. Hawk was an explorer of sorts, always off on some Indiana Jones-like adventure on an exotic island with a name no one could pronounce. In his early fifties, he was nearly ten years her senior, and she liked the age difference. She also liked to joke with him that he was only a part-time private eye because he spent more time away than he did at his small office in the city. He could be counted on to help her see things from a detective's point of view. When it came to investigations, he was an old-fashioned detective just like in the 1940s movies. A few decades older and he could've been an original board game inspiration, except with his brand of detection it would have been *"the phantom in the dining room with a cantaloupe."* She laughed at the thought of an episode in an old satire movie.

He was taller than Alex by at least a foot and ruggedly handsome. She suspected he was also concealing his wealth though they never talked about money, hers or his. Of course, as a private investigator, he could find any information he wanted, but he'd never given her any indication that he was the kind of PI who would pry into a friend's background without cause. He would've considered it a violation of trust and not at all in good taste. Out of all the PIs she'd dealt with, he was the only one not employed by the firm, and because of that, she trusted him completely.

Hawk picked up on the third ring. "Hey there, Al. You enjoying retirement?" he teased.

She loved the rapport but hated when he called her "Al." He was so laid back that sometimes he didn't bother to finish a person's name. *Well, finish my nickname actually.*

"Alex!" she rebuked. "Sadly, it has not been all tea and cakes." She made quick work of explaining the facts of the case to Hawk. It didn't take long to convey the little information she possessed—the neighborhood, the death, the text, the phone number, the notes, and possibly a hit.

"I told you, Lex. There was a lot going on at that firm that you didn't know about. You want me to come to Mass? I can be there in four."

Four hours was what he meant, and he would seriously be there in a beat if she said yes. Hawk had warned her to watch her back when she'd left New York.

His other pet name for her, "Lex," made her grin. It was better than "Al," and she enjoyed the little game they played.

"No. Not yet. Just look into the phone records for me. And if you can, find me a technician or a hacker to get into an old desktop computer circa AOL days."

Laughter sounded through the receiver, but she didn't think *her* joke was that funny.

"I know just the lady for the job. I'll have her call you. She goes by the name 'Le Blanc.' Get it? 'The White'?" he said.

Ah ha! She now understood he wasn't laughing at her joke but rather the one *he* had thought of. His sense of humor was interesting.

"Sure, funny, ha ha. I get it." She smirked. "You know it's not funny if you have to explain it. Seriously, thank you, Hawk," she said and hung up.

Hawk was flawlessly reliable when on a case and perhaps a little sweet on her too. He was the type of guy she could see a future with, a guy her mom would have approved of.

Because it was closer to where she was sitting, she used the back stairwell. Taking the stairs two at a time, she nearly tripped over a stair-step basket beneath the only window in the stairway, an old antique octagon-shaped window. Inside the basket, she found a pair of old binoculars and a small spiral notepad with a pencil threaded through the spiral binding. Nona's handwriting was visible but barely legible as she opened the little notepad. Flipping through all the pages, she was able to piece together what seemed to be a daily routine of random activities. She put the notepad down and picked up the binoculars, intrigued that Nona would be cataloging someone's daily routines. She peered through the window and was dizzied by the unfocused lenses.

A few minor adjustments and she was spying around her backyard. She imagined that Nona must have stood here at least once and watched her and Charlotte as kids, playing in the backyard. Because the window was on the side of the house, she could also see right into Jack's backyard at number 9, a three-story house not quite as large as Alex's and Nona's house.

Nona's son Jack, his wife Sally, their daughter Charlotte, and Nona had lived in number 9 next door to Alex all her childhood. When Nona had moved into Number 1 Spruce Street with Alex, the small Galia family finally had their place to themselves.

Nona had been difficult to live with under normal circumstances. With Nona gone, Sally had been free to raise Charlotte and manage her husband as she saw fit and not how Nona thought Sally should. Sally spoke with Alex just before they made the transition. *If she is too much for you, sweetie, you just let us know.* Alex remembered her words fondly.

"Too much." That was an understatement when it came to describing Nona. Although Nona was tough on Alex—just as she was with everyone else—Alex noticed Nona was more patient with her than she was with most other people.

When Alex had bought her first place in New York City, they'd agreed Nona would stay in the house. It had worked out well for them both. Alex had been able to keep her childhood home in use without guilt of not living in it herself, and Nona could stretch out with her quilting. Nona had hosted the quilt meetings and her book club. The house had been large enough for her to entertain the "biddies."

Alex often thought Nona was a tough woman, simply because of her life experiences. She couldn't imagine having a husband, never mind losing one to the war at just twenty-one years old. Nona had been so madly in love with her husband that she never remarried, thus becoming a single mom to their only child, Jack.

Ultimately, Jack and Sally had divorced after their daughter Charlotte had moved out of the family home. Rather than moving back in with Jack, Nona had stayed in Alex's home at Number 1 Spruce Street.

As Alex kept looking, she could see all the way through the patio door of number 9. The door was closed, but the vertical blinds were open. She could see clearly into the dining room.

Even the fruit bowl full of melons on the table was visible. She turned to look around the yard, embarrassed that she could see so much detail in someone else's home. She instantly lowered the binoculars and ducked in surprise when she saw Jennifer standing to the left of the deck at the compost pile with Kibbles. She stood back up and put her eyes to the binoculars again. Nona had been watching Jennifer? Jack? Both of them?

She wasn't in such a hurry now, with this new information to process—food for thought. After placing the binoculars back in the basket, she put the notepad in her pocket and finished climbing the last five steps to the landing. In her room, she flopped down on the edge of the bed and felt for her familiar princess quilt. It was still in the laundry room. She sagged into her pillows. Multiple actions could have been prevented if Nona had just told her what was going on.

Who had Nona been watching, and what had she been looking for? The little notebook seemed to hold no meaningful clues. Each scribble was a time of the day and what seemed to be ordinary activities: 8:15 am breakfast, 8:45 am left the house, 9:40 am walked Kibbles, 11:45 am lunch, 3:12 pm Betty, 5:50 pm dinner.

She fell asleep thinking she was missing something. There was something here, but she couldn't put her finger on it. What did Jack's and Jennifer's schedule have to do with anything?

After a short siesta, Nona's favorite term, she went back down to the kitchen. She found herself leaning on the sink, blindly staring at the huge fruit basket. Too bad it wasn't one of those ready-to-eat ones she saw advertised on television from Chewable Bouquets.

Pam came into the kitchen. Alex couldn't remember why she'd come down to the kitchen in the first place.

"Pam, did you know about Nona's grass allergy?" she questioned.

"Yes, I assumed you knew too—didn't you?" Pam said, alarmed.

"No, Nona never said a word about it. Look at these. Did you know she received these?" Alex thrust the ominous notes at Pam.

Pam read each one and flipped the papers back and forth. "No" was all she could muster. "But what does this mean?" she finally asked.

"I do not have a clue." Alex shook her head.

"She was acting..." Pam trailed off and went to the sink to wash a few dishes left from the day before.

"Crazed," Alex finished Pam's sentence. "Does this explain all that? Pam, I can get those. You don't have to keep doing that."

"Nonsense," she said with a huff and began to sniffle.

Alex grabbed the box of tissues off the dining room table and handed it to Pam. "Tell me more about this grass pollen allergy. Was it hay fever? Was it serious? Was she overreacting?" she questioned in full defense attorney mode now.

"I don't know." Pam shook her head remorsefully. "She was keeping her hair clean and covered, sunglasses when she went out, keeping the windows closed," Pam said as she looked up at Alex. "You know how she was, 'I don't need anyone to fuss over me. I'm a grown woman,'" Pam mocked Nona's familiar words. "I assumed you knew what was going on. I should've said something."

Alex apologized. "I didn't mean to spring this on you as you are getting ready to leave."

"I can stay a little longer."

"I'm fine. Don't worry. You go take care of your parents." Alex hugged her. "I am so grateful to you for all these years."

When neither of them could stall any longer, Alex saw Pam out. They stood to the side of the street and hugged for a long minute. Alex couldn't help but be overcome. First Nona's death, now Pam was leaving.

Alex watched Pam's car until she could see it turn off Spruce and onto Main Street. She lingered a minute longer and then headed back inside to retrieve her quilt from the dryer.

19

NEVER SEE YOU AGAIN!

SMOOTHING OUT THE WRINKLES, SHE LAID THE QUILT OUT over her bed. Her mind began to work the case again as she started setting up her sewing space in the spare room next to hers.

Betty, Jack ... Doc, Pam ... Alex was going through each of the people in Nona's life who were here on a daily basis and should have known what was going on. Why hadn't anyone filled Alex in on all this?

Next, Alex began making a mental list of people who could have killed Nona. Nona had been frantic about Jack getting married and of Jennifer being the next coming of Satan, but there was never anything to back up her rants about Jennifer, and what motive would either of them have? Jack was her son. He was loving and kind, and even though Nona was threatening to cut him out of the will, they all knew the money was Alex's, so that would be a really weak motive, if one at all.

Betty was her best friend, and there was no sign of a quarrel between them. Could her best friend, her son, or someone in her tightly bound neighborhood really be a killer? Or was it likely that it was the firm? The firm sent someone to kill Alex? Why would they kill Nona? Who would it be? It was nearly impossible for anyone to get around in the neighborhood without the gossip mill knowing and telling.

She was conflicted about so many things. These types of feelings hadn't surfaced since she had been a kid, since her parents had died. Complete control of her life had been her mantra ever since, though Nona had really been in control, hadn't she? This whole week, Alex had found herself out of character—confused, sad, and at a loss. All she really wanted to do was curl up in her bed again and stay there like when she had been fifteen.

She used an elastic to put her hair in a ponytail and put her notepad and pen on top of the dresser. The pad was still blank because she wasn't entirely sure what she was going to do next until she saw the stain from the corner of her eye. It was not much bigger than a nickel in size. She had been sure she had eradicated it.

"What the heck?" she sputtered and yelled at the stain. "The heck with you!"

And your little dog too. She couldn't help but snicker.

"I might not be able to get you out of my quilt, but I can put a patch over you and never see you again!" she continued with the one-sided argument at the persistent stain.

She hustled down the front stairs, nearly missing the last step, which caused her to stumble into the living room door jamb.

"Ow!" she yelped, rubbing her shoulder.

She was just a few feet from the opening to the living room and went straight for Nona's sewing kit in the drawer of the side table, next to the loveseat.

There were about a dozen little sewing kits tucked away throughout the house. Wherever Nona was, she would've been able to work on her quilts. While having tea with the ladies or pie with Betty, there was even a small sewing kit under the lid of the butter dish in the dining room. *No butter in there*, Alex mused.

And the bathroom, she thought, which caused an onslaught of tears. She slumped down into Nona's prized loveseat. She was the only one here, so she didn't need to put on a brave face for appearance's sake.

She patted the arm of the microfiber loveseat. It was by far the ugliest piece of furniture Alex had set her eyes on. It reminded her of a stuffed pig. Shortly after Nona had moved in, a moving company had showed up and delivered it. When Alex had voiced her displeasure, Nona had asked her what a fifteen-year-old knew about interior design. She knew this thing was hideous. That was what she knew. Everyone knew, though over time, they had all grown to appreciate it for its comfort. If nothing else, it was a comfortable loveseat. Smiling, comforted by the thought of something Nona had cherished, Alex pulled herself together. Mentally ready to face the challenge, she smoothed her hair back into her ponytail and dried her eyes.

Finding a teal hexie in the little sewing kit, she pulled out a needle already threaded and tossed the quart-sized Ziploc bag back into the drawer. Not bothering to close the bag or drawer, she took the stairs going back up, more slowly this time. She was determined to rid herself of this stain once and for all. She scrunched up the corner of the quilt, placed the little quarter-sized teal hexagon over the stain, and began to whip stitch it onto her quilt made of wonky stars. *This will certainly add to the wonky.* The thought lifted her mood, and she concentrated on her stitches.

"*Voila!*" she proclaimed with a renewed sense of satisfaction. She tensed for a moment when she realized she had stitched in a bit of Nona to the quilt her mom had made for her.

20

STONE FRUIT PIE

Feeling freed from the stain, she decided to go back to look at the eye spy quilt in the hall closet. Maybe a bit of luck or inspiration would strike, and she would figure out the password to the dinosaur. She checked her phone for texts or voicemails from Hawk, or the white hat hacker, but the screen was void of messages.

In the closet in the front hall, where she had left the quilts that were intended for names and people she didn't know, Alex decided this would be the new stash closet. She certainly wasn't going to parade people in and out of Nona's room.

The late afternoon sun was beaming in through the front door, and she couldn't resist it. Closing the closet door, she headed back upstairs for her sneakers. It was a sunny, warm afternoon, low seventies and no humidity, one of those perfect New England days. It was best to enjoy it out in the rocking chairs. The front porch was a perfect place to hand sew.

On her way up the stairs, she warred with herself on what she should do. If she cozied up on the porch to work on the quilt, she would just spend the time crying in her lap. Maybe a hike would be a better plan to clear her head, think, and figure out what she was missing? Three things were still unresolved: the notes she'd found in Nona's trash can, getting into Nona's computer, and the phone calls that Hawk was looking into.

It was only four o'clock, and there were still a couple hours of daylight left. She wanted to explore the trails and see how the landscape changed or if Nona had requisitioned any new statues. Over the years, Nona had posted signs and added trail markers. Statuaries had been strategically placed in the clearings and on the paths. It had given Nona projects to work on when she'd found herself idle.

Invigorated by the idea of a hike and needing to think on the events surrounding Nona's demise, Alex quickened her pace up the stairs, though she was beginning to feel like a yo-yo going back and forth up and down the stairs so many times already.

She rummaged through her drawers for some comfy pants better suited for a hike and slipped into her sneakers. She squeezed her shoe to check the fit and make sure they were laced up nice and tight, and pocketed her mace. Such a strange thought, needing mace—needing protection at all on Spruce Street.

Finally out on the front porch, she was met by Kibbles, and she could have sworn Jennifer was peeking in the windows. Jennifer held up her plate and shrugged, saying, "Jack reminded me about the plate rack."

"Hey, Kibbles." Alex bent to pet the scruffy dog. "You're not the culprit, are you?" she asked aloud.

She really didn't know if it was a chihuahua or a mix of breeds. She was not a dog person at all and had never owned pets growing up. The one time her mom had brought home a cat, her dad had spent days sneezing and even joked about checking into a hotel. This dog was probably a mutt. A rescue at least—she hoped.

"Kibbles is adorable," Alex continued, scratching the odd-looking dog on the neck. She sort of resembled a teddy bear on legs.

"Where are you headed?" Jennifer asked, startling Alex with her question. "Sorry. It looked like you were on a mission."

"I'm just going for a hike. Try to clear my head. So much has happened this week, and I am trying to put the case together."

Alex stood back up, letting Kibbles wander the porch. *Where's her leash?* she wondered to herself.

"While I have you here, do you eat Sugar Oats cereal?" Alex figured she would chum the waters a bit, and she might as well start with Jennifer. If Nona had been right about Jennifer, there was more to discover behind the empty-headed facade. If she suspected Jennifer was lying, she could confirm it with Jack later.

"No," Jennifer snapped. "Why would you ask that? That's an odd question."

That's an odd response.

Jennifer called for the dog, "Come on, Kibbles, do you want a treat?"

Alex was hoping she wasn't going to feed the dog the disgusting pale gray things in her hand. *Yuck.* But it was enough to get the dog's interest, and she eagerly snatched the little treat from Jennifer's manicured hand. After the dog got its fill of the gross-looking treat, Jennifer scratched Kibbles with her pink daggers, and she trotted off behind Jennifer.

Alex noticed Rigsby wasn't parked out front and assumed Officer Mark was on his way to *camp out.* This whole thing about a hit was absurd. She was certain Officer Mark was over-reacting, or the Feds must be mistaken. She was just about to break into a power walk, past the twins, as Nona referred to Numbers Seven and Five, when she saw Betty in the window of number 5 waving to Alex to come in. Nona had always said the two houses looked like a duplex that had been sawed in half.

Nearly identical Victorian Eclectic houses, just flipped opposite of each other, the two homes were originally built for the daughters of the founder of Salem, John Rogers. The town's history was taught to all the children in elementary school. As the story was told, Rogers originally owned the street, formerly named Conant Court, and he endowed his daughters with houses when they married, so he could keep a close eye on them.

The two houses were now occupied by Fire Chief Cole Cyrus and Officer Mark Cyrus, who lived in number 5 with Blaze, the firehouse's Dalmatian. The two were brothers, and even though Cole was fifteen years Mark's senior, they were both long-time bachelors. The neighborhood folly was that Blaze was the only woman in their lives.

The relationship between Betty and Nona puzzled Alex because the two were polar opposites. Alex trudged up the gravel path between the two houses to Betty's front door.

"Alex, come in for some pie." Betty waved Alex toward the house.

"I was just about to go for a hike, Betty." Alex reluctantly shuffled toward the house. Her original intention was to go for a hike and get some quiet alone time to purge her mind and organize her thoughts. *I might as well use this time to get an update from Betty.*

"Oh, you can spare a few minutes for me. The forest will still be there after pie." Betty looped her arm around Alex's own arm and dragged her inside. "I just made this delicious lemon meringue this morning." Betty's eyes sparkled.

Alex followed her through the entryway and into the kitchen. It was a decent-sized kitchen for a smaller home and well equipped with pie-making paraphernalia. Little chefs danced across the striped valances hanging in the bay window over the sink. The island in the center was a cook's dream, large enough to seat four, with four matching bar stools. Betty pointed

Alex to a small round table and two matching chairs set in a nook on the opposite side. How Alex would have liked to be a fly on the wall in this kitchen. She could just imagine all the gossip that had been spilled at this table over the years.

Alex sat mesmerized by the little chefs, picturing them dancing around the kitchen like in a children's animation. Bowls of fruit ... She was suddenly startled by a realization. *The hexies in Nona's hand? They had to have been part of the eye spy quilt.* She searched her memory for what they looked like. *Food. Fruit. Yes, there is fruit on one of them. Is that random or a clue?* Alex was deep in thought when she heard Betty clear her throat.

"Are you listening to me, Alex? I said today is the perfect day for lemon meringue. Not too humid." Betty grinned.

"Yes, Betty, thank you." She was up to her meddling ways, Alex could tell. Alex wasn't sure she should eat anything Betty gave her. "As long as you will join me."

"Of course. I would love a slice of pie. I hear it's very good." Betty winked. "I saw Officer Mark stop by earlier. And Rigsby, why was she parked in front of number 1 earlier?"

Wow, she didn't waste any time. Alex reminded herself to let Betty do all the talking, and she would get whatever clues Betty offered.

"Was he investigating the notes Nona received?" Betty asked.

"What—" Alex tried to get a question in, but Betty kept on talking.

"Was he looking into Jennifer because she threatened her?"

"Jennifer threatened Nona?" Alex's voice was a little louder than she meant it to be.

"Well, maybe Nona was threatened *by her*? Either way, she was watching her, you know."

Alex interrupted Betty this time and asked, "Jennifer was watching Nona?"

"No. Nona was watching Jennifer."

Alex already suspected this because of the binoculars and notepad.

"Betty, do you know why? What was she expecting to see?"

"I don't know, Alex. Nona never told me what she was looking for."

"What do you know about the notes, Betty?"

"She told me what the notes said. I told her to go to the police. Did she?"

"No, Betty. I don't think she did. I found the notes crumpled up in her trash can. Today, as a matter of fact."

"Did you notice there has been a serious increase in traffic on the street since Jennifer moved in? You know she gets a delivery every few days? Probably those awful Lularun leggings that she wears. Tacky," Betty tsked.

Alex could envision Nona saying those exact words.

"I was making a stone fruit pie yesterday," Betty babbled. "You know, they can be a bit tricky if you don't keep an eye on them. Anyway, I think I finally saw the guy in number 13, but by the time I got the pie out of the oven, he was gone."

No one had a visual on the new neighbor in number 13 yet, except for Betty and possibly Nona because she had been snooping around before Alex had come home to Spruce Street.

"Have some lemon meringue." Betty shoved a huge helping of pie in front of Alex and set down a glass of milk. Betty took a seat at the small table, directly across from Alex, with a significantly smaller piece of pie and a glass of milk.

Alex waited for Betty to take the first bite of pie before she dug into hers. Betty resumed, "Some people put in too many fruits. Not me. Cherries, peaches, and plums, that's it. That's my secret to making a great stone fruit pie." With a serious face, she said, "Don't tell anyone, Alex."

Gosh, Betty's pies were out-of-this-world delicious. There

was no denying that. Alex sighed as she rounded the last bite of the lemon meringue she hadn't even intended on eating.

"Good, finish up that pie. You are too skinny," Betty remarked. "I don't put any melons in mine. That's just personal preference."

Alex leaned back. She hadn't been keeping up and really should have been paying more attention.

"And besides, they're not even stone fruits," she added as an afterthought. Betty grinned and stood, holding out her hand for the empty plate. Staring out the kitchen window, she continued absently, "You know, Pete has a nice apple tree in his yard. I think I'll make another apple crisp tonight." Coming back to her senses, she said, "Well, you are going to need that hike now, Alex." She turned and waved toward the front door. "That was a big piece of pie you ate."

She had never understood why Nona was best friends with Betty. She was a bit fruity, no pun intended. Alex wasn't a huge fan of the lady. Her pies sure, but Betty, not so much. In a matter of a single slice of pie, she had been insulted twice and learned a bunch of nothing about a pie she had never even heard of.

Alex stood. She took her cue to shoo before Betty got started again. She was full from the meringue, but she could burn it off on her hike.

"By the way, Betty, do you eat Sugar Oats cereal?"

"I don't eat cereal at all. Too sweet. I only buy a few boxes here and there, so I can give them to Nona for her templates. I feed the cereal to the birds in Pete's yard." She winked. "Don't tell him!"

Alex thanked Betty for the pie and saw herself out. As she was leaving, she could hear Betty murmuring something about the birds.

21

NUTHATCHES

OUT ON THE STREET, ALEX BEGAN HER STRIDE FOR THE entrance to the woods, which was about halfway down the street. Two more houses to go, she thought. Number 11, the next house on the street was a simple Cape-style house, the last one built on the street, at the same time as number 13. It was owned by Lucy, the town's clerk, and her husband, Pete.

"Alex. Hey, Alex," she heard from over her shoulder.

She stopped and then realized it was too late now. Why had she stopped? To her dismay, Pete was flagging her down.

From the street, Alex could see Pete was making another of his elaborate birdhouses. He was the neighborhood handyman and the male version of Betty.

Good grief, both of them in one day, Alex thought. She wanted to make a run for it. The entrance to the path was so close, just a couple hundred feet down, across the street.

She stopped, turned, and greeted Pete. "Hi." She waved as she drifted down the paved driveway to where he was standing by the two-car garage that sported the number 11.

"How do you like my new masterpiece?" he asked, as he motioned to the gigantic birdhouse. It was the size of a small dog house but with dozens of holes for birds. It was intricately decorated with wooden trim like a doll house.

"This is something, Pete." She moved closer to get a good look. "How many hours go into making something like this?" She was genuinely curious.

"Oh, it's nothing. It is a labor of love. Lucy loves the birds, and I love woodworking ... and Lucy, of course. I use these tiny nails on all the trim." He held up a nail and the hammer to show Alex how small they were.

"Those are really small nails," Alex responded awkwardly. She felt like she was in an episode of *The Truman Show*.

"Say, you haven't been to that new salon across town, have you? I mean to get your nails done?" he asked and gestured toward her hand.

"No." *Strange question,* she thought as she unconsciously looked down at her badly worn French manicure. "Why do you ask?"

"Lucy heard from Ann who heard from Cole not to go there. Something about Jennifer losing a nail and getting an infection? These little nails, you know, made me think of it," he said shyly. "You know how the gals can get when they gab."

"I do," she replied. "Thank you for letting me know. That reminds me, do you or Lucy eat Sugar Oats cereal?"

"No, we eat oatmeal. Every morning. Keeps you regular." He chortled. "Anyway, I made this new box for the white-breasted nuthatches. This is the first time we've seen them here in the neighborhood. I wanted to make them feel welcome," he said earnestly.

The residents of Spruce Street are anything but regular, and it is definitely not the first time we've seen nuthatches on Spruce Street.

"Speaking of nuthatches, watch out for the nut next door. He's been in rare form lately. I can hear him puttering around the yard crabbing to himself. He's been going on about 'murder and mayhem'!" Pete grinned.

Clearly, he hadn't gotten the memo yet! Alastor was right to be going on about murder and mayhem. This was an unprecedented time for Spruce Street.

"*Fumbo.*"

"What's '*fumbo*'?" Alex asked.

"I think it means '*mystery*' in Swahili," Pete answered. "Well, at least that's what the Google showed me when I typed it in." He laughed.

Alex couldn't help herself as she laughed, too, shaking her head at Pete. *The Google.*

"Pete, it's always a pleasure talking to you. I'm going to run, though. I want to get a hike in before it gets dark."

"Okay, I'll see you, Alex." He turned back to his little hammer and tiny nails. "Be wary of the *fumbo*," he called back as she was almost out of earshot.

"I will," she muttered.

22

FUMBO

She looked to her right, and there was no sign of Alastor Arnold, the neighborhood grouch at number 3, an adorable gingerbread-style Victorian house. He created a barrier to the rest of the neighborhood by partially hiding the house behind a six-foot wooden fence. Just past the fence to Alastor's backyard, and she would be able to cross the street to the entrance to the forest. She could enter now through a patch of thinner trees or go in through the main entrance.

As she quietly snuck past the fence, Alastor was muttering on the other side. *"Machafuko,"* she heard. *"Vurugu."* He was repeating the two words over and over.

What does that mean? she wondered. *And why is he speaking in Swahili, if Pete was right about what he heard?*

He was a difficult man and the last person she wanted to encounter right now.

"Alex, is that you?" she heard.

How did he know she was there? He couldn't possibly have heard her. She was basically tiptoeing, and he was behind a six-foot wooden fence.

"Come here, girl. I want to talk to you," Alastor called to her through the fence.

She hung her head in resignation. She'd dealt with some pretty nutty people as a lawyer in the city, but she was beginning to wonder if they were no match for the residents of Spruce Street.

She huffed and advanced to the edge of the fence, past the entrance to the forest. "Hi, Alastor. What can I do for you today?"

"Nona told me you were coming for a visit. I suppose you'll be staying now?" he questioned.

"Yes, that's right. I am here to stay." *Little late on the neighborhood gossip.*

Alastor grumbled, "My brother was going to come and stay, too, but he won't, now that Nona has passed. It's better off, really. We really didn't need a *savior* on Spruce Street."

"Ooh-kay." What was up with her neighbors? She wondered if they had all gone insane, or was it just her? Was she supposed to know what the heck he was talking about?

She might as well ask him too. "Alastor, do you eat Sugar Oats cereal?"

"I meet the guys at Rise and Grind every morning at 6:00 a.m., sharp. Almond biscotti and a black coffee, ask that kid."

"Joey?" she asked.

"Yes, he knows my order." Alastor stood back looking dubious.

"That's okay, I believe you." She responded with a forced smile. "I was just about to go for a hike." She thumbed over her shoulder in the general direction of the woods. "About forty-five minutes ago," she thought as she looked at her watch.

"Yeah, yeah, go." He dismissed her and turned away.

As she hustled out of the yard, she couldn't stop from thinking maybe she should just head back to number 1, crawl under the covers, and stay in bed, as she'd originally wanted to do in the first place.

She intended to interrogate her neighbors at some point, but at this rate, maybe it was best left up to the police. She couldn't imagine trying to have legitimate conversations about anything serious with any of these people. Well, if she took it on face value, she ruled out Alastor, Pete, Lucy, Betty ... and possibly Jennifer for the cereal box note. She was definitely going to ask Jack, just to confirm.

Her phone buzzed with a text from Hawk.

The # traced back to Walpole, Mass.
2 things in that location.
Pay phone at abandoned gas station and a prison.

23

WHICH PATH?

Alex called Hawk back immediately but hung up when it went straight to his voicemail.

A familiar sign caught her eye as she entered the path to the woods. It was a rough plank of old wood nailed to a tree. "Spruce Street Hiking Trails," it read. Nona had commemorated the purchase with the sign. At the time, Alex had thought it was impetuous. Alex had suggested to Nona that people might get the wrong idea.

"Nonsense. We'll just tell anyone who dares question it that it was our victory over *the man*." She had cackled so hard her false teeth had flinched.

At the time, Alex had been seriously hoping Nona wasn't going to go off the deep end and turn into a suffragette. *More like a fruit bat,* Alex quipped, remembering the conversation.

The twenty-acre wooded plot had been slated for development just after Alex had started law school. Nona had called Alex at college to let her know she wasn't going to stand for her street being developed. She'd insisted something needed to be done to stop the development, and Alex couldn't believe what Nona wanted *her* to do. She shouldn't have been surprised, really. *Riffraff,* she mused at what Nona called the potential intrusion of new neighbors.

We can't let the riffraff in. You have to buy the street, had been her declaration.

At the time, Alex hadn't known how much it cost to buy a street or if someone could even do such a thing. Despite Nona's screwball idea, because that is exactly what Alex thought of it at the time, with Celia's help, Alex had done just as Nona had asked her to. She had bought the right-hand side of Spruce Street. Well, the anonymous company, ANB Inc., bought the street, on paper anyway. Celia Moore, the local real estate agent, had negotiated the purchase. Alex, Nona, and Celia were the keepers of the secret—this secret anyway.

Alex remembered the conversation like it was just yesterday. *You wanted it, Nona, and now, it's yours! What are you going to do with half a street?*

Nothing, leave it just as it is. No one ever has to know, were her final words on the matter, although they both knew it wouldn't stay a secret forever, especially on Spruce Street.

Of course, Nona had seized the opportunity to call Alex, at the time, to fill her in on the buzz. The neighborhood gossip was ablaze after the construction company mysteriously packed up and went away. No one else had known what had transpired.

We happened, that's what! Nona had exclaimed.

Speculation had been rampant, and Alex had heard it all from Nona, everything from mafia connections, con men, scandalous affairs, and even money laundering. None of which held any merit, of course. Alex's life had never been dull when it had come to Nona. Nona got what she wanted, and to this day, no additional houses had been built on her street. The forest and trails were safe, and so was their secret.

Alex headed into the woods along the main path. She was invigorated by the warmth of the sun, the woodsy resinous smell of the pine and spruce trees, and the chance to ground herself. Her emotions swung like a pendulum, especially today.

She came to the old wooden bench in the small clearing where the trails branched off in multiple directions and Nona had planted a small wildflower garden. The floral scents were delicate but not shy. There was a small box attached to a metal stake in the ground that held a poop bag dispenser. A small trash can was screwed into the stake. The dispenser read, "Pick up your crap!"

Just like Nona. Alex choked out a laugh.

Each path was marked with wooden signs on four-foot-tall posts made from rough lumber and buried into the ground. The signs were pointed on one end, facing the direction of travel, and the path distances were hand-painted on each one. Pete had made the signs and paced off the distances. The counts were pretty accurate, given the lack of modern technology at the time.

Contemplating how far she wanted to hike, Alex perched on the worn bench for a few minutes, "hike" being a loose term, as the elevation didn't change very much. The land was fairly flat across most of the property, which made it ideal for building and subsequently costing Alex a small fortune to procure.

At her feet, fresh scuff marks reminded her of the letter box she and Charlotte hid under the bench when they were kids. Letterboxing had become very popular in the eighties. The girls had learned of it as a school project in Ms. Melo's class. Alex had made sure to check on it the last time she'd come home also, so she knew it was still there. She got down on her hands and knees, and something sharp bit into her hand. A small piece of pink plastic.

"Ouch." She rubbed her palm. Thankfully, her skin was not broken.

She pulled out the small weatherproof box. Inside, a plastic Ziploc baggie held a small spiral notepad, a small stamp, an inkpad, and a pencil. The spiral notepad was the third or fourth incarnation. She couldn't remember exactly what the riddle or clues were anymore that led the public to the Spruce Street box, but over the years, hundreds of kids and adults had found the box and signed or stamped the little notepads. As the little notepads had filled up, Alex or Nona had exchanged them for new ones. The little stamp was of a single Spruce Tree in a perfect conifer shape, and the inkpad was green, of course. She carefully opened the little notepad and flipped through the delicate pages with familiar entries. There were hers, of course, but also Charlotte and Nona's, which were written at the front of each book.

She longingly rubbed her fingers over the writing. Over the years, people had ventured in to find the letter box and left their own stamps on the notepad—a dragonfly, a tiny house with just four walls and a roof, a few different Salem-esque stamps like witches, black cats, and ghosts, and even a couple that were unrecognizable, most likely hand-carved stamps that held meaning to the person who left them. Most were simply a name and a stamp, though some were dated.

Alex flipped toward the back, looking for a clean page. She found the last two stamps, and both were dated just last week. On the left was a little blue quilt block with a hand holding a sewing needle. She could even make out a little thin line for the thread on Nona's stamp. She wiped at her eyes with her sleeve as the tears began to well up in the corners. She hadn't thought to bring tissues along for the hike. She hadn't expected to need them. She should've realized this would be emotional. Alex stamped her own little tree stamp underneath Nona's quilt block and wrote her own name and the date.

The stamp on the right was a little dog with the name "Ray." It seemed Nona had been here recently and with someone. Someone named Ray? *The same Ray that Officer Mark asked me about? But how could Lucas Ray stamp the little notepad? He's in jail!*

Nervous, she tucked the notebook and contents back in the box. She got down on the ground to replace the box in its hiding place under the bench.

The decision was made. She would take the path through the center. It was a direct route, in and back again, in a fairly straight line. It would be easy to follow, and she wouldn't have to pay attention to the trail markers or risk getting turned around and ending up out after dark.

I CAN SEE YOU

Alex shivered at the possibility of how a former client of hers, who was in jail, could have stamped the little notepad. She tried in vain to organize her thoughts and feelings about her career with Weitz & Romano, coming home to Spruce Street, and all that had transpired over the last few days. When she'd left the law firm in New York City, she'd thought she was freeing herself from the corruption and escaping to a more peaceful way of life.

While deep in thought, her phone buzzed, and she saw it was Officer Mark's personal cell. She swiped to answer the call.

Alex heard a crunching noise behind her and turned automatically to see who was there.

Jennifer, in bright orange Lularun pants.

Jennifer stopped mid-stride, and Alex watched her do the strangest thing. She stood and held her position. Her arms were held at odd angles, one up and one down, and her legs awkwardly spread apart. It looked as if she was trying to be a tree and blend in with the surroundings.

"What are you doing, Jennifer?" Alex asked.

Jennifer didn't respond.

"I can see you," Alex said, shaking her head. She walked back in the direction toward Jennifer. Alex stopped short. A sunbeam gleamed through the trees and bounced off something metal. A metal blade. A knife in Jennifer's right hand. As Alex got close, she saw Jennifer was brandishing a cleaver.

"Stop right there, Alex." Her voice no longer held any "*nice-girl*" pretense.

"What do you plan on doing with that knife, Jennifer?"

Jennifer advanced a single step toward Alex, and Alex stopped automatically in response and put her hand in her pocket.

"Jennifer, ha! That's not even my real name. I'm surprised that a big city, golden girl lawyer could be so daft. This isn't even my real hair!" she screamed and ripped off her bouffant hair, throwing her wig on the ground and revealing a dirty blonde pixie haircut.

Alex was stunned into silence, for Jennifer had transformed from bizarre to unstable in a blink. Without the wig Alex was finally able to place Jennifer's face. The face she had been trying to remember was not of a woman she'd met before. *This face* had an uncanny resemblance to *a man she had known* —*Lucas Ray*.

"Why don't you tell me what's going on here, Jennifer?"

"Oh, I'll tell you exactly what's going on!" Jennifer screamed back at Alex. "It's you or us! That's what's going on!"

"Let's stay calm. I don't understand what you're talking about, Jennifer. Who is '*us*?'"

"I like you, Alex, but when you asked me about the Sugar Oats cereal, I knew you were on to me. The new outfit hired me to get this job done." Jennifer's resolve softened. "And I'm out of time."

Who is 'us'? Who is she working with? The person who sent the text? That couldn't be. The text was a warning, not a threat.

"Jennifer, can you try to explain to me what's going on here? What don't you have a choice about? Who is '*us*'?"

Jennifer scoffed, "Ninety-eight and one and you couldn't figure this out. You've really made this too easy for me." She waved the cleaver around to emphasize the '*this*'. "My name's not Jennifer."

The woman standing in front of Alex was no longer the flighty, ditzy woman she had impressed upon the neighborhood. Her pixie haircut was standing in all directions from when she'd ripped the wig off, and she looked like a small porcupine was claiming her head as its home. The knife in her hand was serious, but Alex was having a hard time taking her seriously.

"What's your real name? Maybe I can help you. I am a lawyer. I know people. If you are in trouble, I can help you," Alex assured her.

Shoving the cleaver in Alex's direction, she snarled, "Oh, you know people all right. That's what got you into this situation in the first place. Your firm! I don't really know what I'm doing. I've never killed anyone before. It was just a little side hustle in Las Vegas."

The pieces of the puzzle were starting to fall into place, and Alex realized it must have been Jennifer who wrote the two notes. Las Vegas, LVR.

"L-V-R—those are *your* initials?"

I AM COMING FOR YOU! —LVR
YOU'RE GOING TO NEED YOUR LAWYER

"Yes, the 'Las Vegas Rays' they called us back home. It was just a side hustle. Lucas was never meant to get involved. He was in over his head. We were never meant to get involved with the family."

Alex wasn't listening. She was busy thinking about how Nona had been right about Jennifer all along.

"My name is Lilith Violet Ray. Do you recognize me? Have you placed my face yet?"

Alex knew the connection. *Lucas Ray.*

Alex hadn't recognized her, despite that nagging feeling that Jennifer was familiar to her in some way. It was simply her close resemblance to Lucas Ray. Alex's client. Jennifer's, or rather, Lilith's, twin.

Furthering her rant, Lilith exclaimed, "My brother! My brother, Lucas Ray. LVR, Lucas Vaughn Ray. My twin! He didn't deserve to go to prison! I'm running out of time to get this job done." She sneered and advanced forward again in Alex's direction a few steps. "We were happy in Las Vegas, doing our own thing, until we got mixed up with you and your law firm and Lucas went to jail."

Alex couldn't afford to let her get any closer if she was going to have any chance to escape this psycho. Alex stepped backward again, now she was inches from touching the large Spruce tree behind her. She had nowhere else to go.

25

LIKE YOU HELPED BEFORE

"Don't move!" Lilith demanded.

Alex put her left hand up in defense. At this point, all she could do was stall her as long as possible and get as much of the story as she could.

Pointing the gleaming cleaver at Alex, Lilith told her, "My brother is in prison because of you and your firm, but we have a chance. He can get out, and this can all be over. He is the only family I have."

Alex put her hand up in defense again. "Easy now!"

Her brother, Lucas Ray, was the one. Ninety-eight wins and one loss, the one case that Alex hadn't won. The one case she should've won. The one case where she had believed the defendant was actually innocent. There was nothing Alex could've done for Lucas. With Judge Sterne on the bench, Lucas hadn't stood a chance.

All these years, Alex had suffered from the regret of not being able to help Lucas. She knew he wasn't squeaky clean, but he was a good kid. An innocent kid. He didn't deserve to go to jail for someone else's, i.e. Lilith's, crimes. That had been one of the biggest reasons Alex had finally decided to leave the firm and come back to Spruce Street. She had wanted to rid herself of the stain of nearly ten years of fighting for the wrong side.

"Even if you kill me, they won't let Lucas out of jail, Jennifer."

"Lilith. My name is Lilith!" she shouted and advanced on Alex again.

One more half-step, and Alex was backed against the tree. She could feel a low-hanging branch grazing the top of her head.

"Okay, Lilith. They won't let Lucas go. He won't get out of prison. You have to know this. Let me help you."

Lilith scoffed. "Like you helped my brother! Ha! No thanks! I'll take my chances. I've made it this far. They have their ways. They promised me he would get out." Despite her words, she looked down as her confidence in her own plan wavered for a split second.

Alex stepped forward.

Lilith countered step for step in Alex's direction. "They told me exactly where your precious, beloved mayor was going to be in Las Vegas. With the wig"—she pointed the cleaver in the direction of the wig—"and these"—she cupped her large breasts —"it was easy to seduce him. Oh, his buddies egged him on. It wasn't a tough sell. He jumped at the chance to marry a cute little button fifteen years younger than him," she said with a laugh. "He followed the pattern perfectly and brought me back to this crazy neighborhood." Lilith waved the cleaver around again signifying the neighborhood. "And I placed my bait ... the notes." She stood bristling and proud. "Get the fancy lawyer. Check," Lilith said, waving the cleaver in the air in a check mark motion. "I faked a burglary and a few warnings, and the old lady got her lawyer here like I intended." She paused for a moment of consciousness. "It's too bad about Nona, but she wouldn't leave well enough alone." Lilith sneered. "I clipped that thread too. The way she was going around town telling everyone I was bad news, she was going to get me caught. None of that was part of my plan, but I took care of her!"

Alex nearly doubled over from the pain of the thought of Nona's death being her fault, but she knew, as in Lucas's case, it had been Lilith's actions that had led them all to this point, not Alex's.

"I gotta give her credit. Nona was on to me. She forced me to be creative. I tried to get her with the tea at first."

Alex remained silent. Like most people with logorrhea, Lilith laid it all out. Alex could hardly believe that just a week ago, all had seemed normal, and it had subsequently escalated to this. Lilith blamed it all on Alex, and there was a whiff of truth to that, but Alex wasn't the one responsible for getting Lucas mixed up in illegal activity. The realization dawned on Alex that it was Lilith that Lucas was protecting all this time. *Lilith* was the one the Feds wanted to catch, and *she* was the reason they'd made an example of Lucas.

If Hawk worked the case, they wouldn't have missed all this. Alex shook her head at the thought.

As long as Lilith didn't start waving that cleaver at Alex again, Alex was confident that she would be able to get away, and patience was one of Alex's favorite tools. She was the one being *creative* now. Plus, she did have the mace spray in her pocket.

"Are you putting the clues together yet, fancy, big city lawyer?" Lilith taunted her.

Alex shook her head no. She needed to get Lilith to reveal exactly how she'd killed Nona.

"Grass. I started with the tea. Isn't it obvious for someone who has a grass allergy?" Lilith was dead serious. "I was beginning to think maybe I was actually good at this!" she shook her head back and laughed hard. After she composed herself again, she mocked, "This neighborhood!" She shook her head again, this time in disbelief. "Doc telling you and Jack it was an allergic reaction. That was priceless. He was right, of course. It was." She cocked her head and then uttered, "But not how you think!"

There was still a missing piece to the puzzle, and Alex was confident she was going to get all the evidence she needed right here from Lilith's own admission.

"Well, what was it?" Alex asked plainly.

"Oh, you people think I'm a ditzy bimbo, but I'll have you know I have a college degree. From a real college!" she declared and shook the cleaver for emphasis.

Alex was dumbfounded that this lunatic—scratch that, that this lunatic "with a brain"—had schemed and killed Nona to get at Alex and that she thought she was going to get away with it.

"As it turns out, it was cantaloupe that did her in!" Lilith straightened her posture, proud as a peacock.

"Cantaloupe?" Alex asked, truly puzzled by this. It was an elaborate plan, so elaborate that Alex almost didn't believe Lilith.

"Yes, this is where Lady Luck was on my side. You see, I researched this 'grass' allergy, the way she was going to the salon daily, having her hair washed, and wearing those ridiculous scarfs and oversized sunglasses. What a kook." Lilith snickered. "Absurd if you ask me."

It was pretty absurd, Alex admitted to herself, but apparently Nona had taken the allergy seriously.

"At first, I tried throwing the landscapers off their schedule and opening her window. She led me right into her bedroom to pick out fabric from her special 'stash' closet, and I saw the EpiPen there. I figured the landscapers might just do the job for me." She looked at Alex with regret in her eyes. "But it didn't work." Her eyes squished. "It was the strangest thing. Anyway, I'm going to kill you, so I might as well let you in on my genius.

Once I kill you, I'll be *in* with the family, but maybe the firm will hire me too, for my ingenuity!" she bragged.

What did she mean by that? Why would the law firm hire her?

"After multiple tries, I began to think maybe it wasn't really a grass allergy at all. I went to work researching ways to kill someone with a grass allergy, and as it turns out, people who have grass allergies can have other rare allergies. Apples ... melons ... I knew she wasn't allergic to apples because big-mouth Betty told me they were having apple crisp every morning." Lilith relaxed a fraction as she took pride in her accomplishments. "The two of them were probably trying to figure out my plan, so I gambled on the melon allergy. I'm pretty confident she didn't have a grass allergy," Lilith added, "but I am no doctor, so I made her a nice tea loaf."

"But you said the tea didn't work?" Alex was infuriated with this woman. "You're a murderer!" she hollered.

"Well, yes, yes, I am. To help my precious brother get out of jail, I'll do anything, including a bit of spring cleaning! The whole thing is pretty *cray cray*, if you think about it, but the melon was worth a try. If it didn't work, in the worst case, I would just try something more direct." She started laughing. "Ha, you know what the best part of this whole plan was? When you delivered the tea loaf for me. It stood to reason that if you ate it, she would eat it too."

That was an unexpected punch to the gut. Alex's stomach wretched, and bile rose in her throat.

"Didn't see that one coming? Turns out you didn't get her to eat it." Lilith frowned, "when I came by the next night, she must've felt guilty because we ate the loaf," Lilith mused, stepping closer in Alex's direction again.

Lilith better hurry, or Alex might not be able to get out of this. Alex was going to need to think of a distraction before Lilith finished her montage.

"Spiced tea loaf is what I told you it was. I couldn't tell you what it really was just in case that old bag knew about the possibility of a melon allergy. I wouldn't have put it past her," Lilith quipped. "Google the recipe, Alex. Spiced 'cantaloupe' tea loaf. Would you have ever guessed that?" She began to laugh hysterically. "The clues were all there, right along."

2 6

CHECK

When Lilith was calm long enough to speak without laughing, she continued her tirade, "Well, I guess you won't be able to Google it. You'll have to take my word for it. It's really too bad about Jack. He was very nice to me. I think maybe in another life, I could've doubled down and let it ride. But my brother, he needs me to get him out of this..." she trailed off and straightened up.

Lilith looked Alex right in the eyes.

Here we go. Alex could see she was steeling up the nerve to do what she had come here to do.

"I won't let him down!" she yelled and charged forward, pointing the cleaver directly at Alex's head.

Alex ducked just in time to miss a cleaver to the eye.

Lilith wrestled with the cleaver now stuck in the tree, as Alex switched positions with her.

Much like her trying to *"be a tree"* hiding in the woods, she wasn't very good at this part of murder either. Lady Luck would be on Alex's side this time. The mammoth tree gripped the weapon, and Lilith's only play was a *miss*!

Lilith turned to Alex in shock and put her fists up. She watched as Alex lifted her hand to her face.

"Did you get all that, Mark?" she asked.

"Yes, I'm just at the entrance to the woods now. Are you all right?" he asked.

"Yes," Alex said, hanging up the phone. She stepped aside as Officer Mark came into the path with his service weapon locked on Lilith.

"Are you sure you are okay, Alex?"

"My brother! He'll die in prison," Lilith pleaded with Officer Mark as he cuffed her.

Officer Mark led Lilith out of the woods towards his squad car, and Alex followed a safe distance behind. They were met on the street by several Spruce Street residents, cheering on Officer Mark and Alex.

"Geez, word sure does travel fast on Spruce Street!" Mark shouted over the commotion.

"It sure does!" Alex agreed.

Officer Mark ducked Lilith into the back of his police car.

Before he closed the door, Alex crouched down so Lilith could hear what she was about to say. Alex just couldn't help herself. "Catch the bad guy. Check."

DESTINATIONS

Alex spent the next two days in and out of the police station, going over everything in detail with Officer Mark. She gave her account of the events that had transpired on Spruce Street since she had returned home. She also met with a detective and an agent who came in from New York City to protect Alex and investigate her past employers' involvement.

She decided to withhold the curious warning text. Something in her gut was telling her not to trust the Feds with this piece of information. She saved that for Hawk.

Today, the three items on her agenda were to file the paperwork at Lucy's office, then pick up the new car she had purchased online, and, with any luck, there would be time to finally get over to Destinations, the local travel/real estate agency. She needed to meet with Celia to pick up the package Nona had bestowed upon Celia. In all the excitement, her conversation with Celia, and the package awaiting her, had slipped her mind.

After picking up her new car from the dealership across town, she headed back toward Destinations. She made it just in time, with about ten minutes to spare until Celia would be closing up.

"I'm sorry I'm late, Celia," Alex said.

"It's no problem, I have a client coming for a second showing on a split ranch across town, but he's not due here for a little while yet. We've got time," Celia said as she looked at her watch. "I'll be right back." She disappeared into her office for no more than a minute. She came out holding a large manila envelope.

Alex gave her a questioning look as she took the envelope from Celia. After everything that had happened during the past week, she wasn't sure she wanted any more surprises.

"It better be good," Alex commented, eyeing Celia ruefully.

Alex's name was written on the front in Nona's scrolled handwriting. Inside the large envelope were four smaller sealed envelopes. The top one, a white letter-size envelope, also displayed Alex's name scrolled across the front, then another manila envelope also with Alex's name on it and two more letter-size envelopes with Jack and Charlotte's names on them.

Alex fell into the chair beside Celia's desk. There were so many questions, "H-How? When? What?" she stammered, trying to pick one that made the most sense, but finding none.

Celia looked at her sweetly and shrugged and simply said, "Nona." Celia set a box of tissues and a letter opener down on the edge of the desk. "I'll leave you with these. I have some calls to make, and I'll come back in and check in on you in a few minutes."

Celia darted into her office. She was so quick Alex didn't

have time to register a protest or ask any further one-word questions.

Alex took a deep breath, steeled herself, picked up the letter opener, and opened the first envelope with her name on it

My best girl Alex,

I have loved you like a daughter, and even though you came into our family under tragic circumstances, you have brought me such joy all these years. I have been so proud of you and all of your achievements. So proud! You deserve all the happiness in the world!

If you are reading this, sadly, I was right about my son's no-good, vile wife! I know that I did all I could for the neighborhood and our family all these years.

I am glad you came back to Spruce Street. There is a lot of work to be done now. You will have to take over in my absence. You will find a second envelope with your name on it. Inside are cruise tickets.

Yes, you read that right.

They're tickets for everyone on Spruce Street.

Yes, you read that right too!

I want Ann Melo to join you. She has loved my son Jack since they were in diapers. I just know they are meant to be together. You can help with that.

Bring Joey if he can spare the time away from his studies. It might be one of the few chances he gets to have some fun before going off into the world. Look after him, will you? I know you will.

Oh, and DO NOT forget to bring Henrietta! It's important.

By now, I know you are thinking I've completely gone off the deep end. I haven't. I assure you.

Celia will handle all the remaining travel details. Your job

is to make sure all of our friends and family make it on the ship. I am sure you have asked me "where" several times already reading this, but "where" the ship is headed is not the important part. It's the journey.

You are the new mother of Spruce Street. Relax. I'll always be here to guide you.

Alex flipped the page, eager that the words not stop.

Just go! Don't make a case about it. You deserve something nice for yourself, Alex. You have worked so hard and been so successful, and I know your cases have taken a toll on you. Cleanse yourself of all that.

It's time for you to enjoy your life. You have the means! Take our family and friends on a vacation and just have fun!
—Nona

Alex sank, laughing and weeping, the tears streaming down her face uncontrollably.

Even from the grave, Nona was the boss.

She tore open the second envelope with her name on it, and sure enough, there was a stack of cruise ship tickets, a ticket for each member of the family and all their friends on Spruce Street. Even tickets for Joey and Ms. Melo.

On cue Celia came back in with another box of tissues.

"How?" Alex asked.

"If I would have known that something awful was going to happen to her..." Celia dabbed at her face with a tissue. "I didn't know, Alex. I just thought she was doing something nice for everyone. I never imagined it would be her last request," Celia stated and started sobbing.

Alex put her hand on Celia's arm. There was nothing to be said, aloud anyway.

Alex lingered, contemplating Nona's last request. How on earth could she expect a whole neighborhood of people to go on a cruise together?

Celia's client came in and interrupted Alex mid-thought. They both got up and embraced, and Celia excused herself to her client. A few minutes later, she was back and as professional as Alex had ever seen her.

Alex let herself out with the envelopes and tickets in hand, wondering how she was going to pull this off. How she was going to fill Nona's shoes as the "new mother" of Spruce Street.

When she got into her new BMW—yeah, she'd splurged, she figured she owed it to herself—she used the hands-free to call Charlotte and Jack and asked them to meet her at number 1 later in the evening, so she could deliver Nona's letters to them.

When Jack and Charlotte arrived separately, Alex could see Charlotte was fuming.

"I don't know why we're here. I haven't been able to reconcile this whole fiasco. I'm glad you caught her Alex, I am … but I'm really upset with the both of you. You brought this woman into our lives," Charlotte said with an accusatory stare at Alex.

There was nothing Alex could say. No apology or reasoning was going to replace the fact that Charlotte's grandmother was gone, and she had every right to be upset. Alex wasted no time and simply handed the letters to each of them and sat down on the loveseat. She was still puzzled by her own letter as she sat back and watched Charlotte and Jack read their letters.

A fresh box of tissues was at the ready as Charlotte read her letter.

Charlotte,

My only granddaughter. I have been tough on you all these years, I know. It is only because I love you and I wanted the very best for you. What I've come to realize is, it is your life to live as you want.

You are a wonderful woman capable of great things, and all I want is for you to be happy ... and wealthy in life, like your father!

—Your loving Nona

Charlotte looked up quickly, and Alex shrugged. "*Nona,*" she mouthed silently.

Jack scoffed as he began to read.

Jack,

It's your mother.

If you are reading this letter, I was right!

Jack couldn't believe his eyes. "T-That woman," he stammered as he stared at the empty page. "That's it?" He flipped the letter over, hoping for more, and was rewarded.

Ha—got ya!

Sorry, I couldn't resist.

In all seriousness. If you are reading this, then I was right about that floozy Jennifer, and I'm sorry I couldn't protect you from her.

It's true I loved your first wife, Sally, dearly, but I've always wanted you to be happy. I hoped you and Sally were for life, but I do understand that things didn't work out as planned, and I was sad to see you alone all these years.

Recently, I finally realized it was time for you to be with Ann Melo. She's been in love with you since you two were in diapers. It broke my heart to see you come home with a new bride. After all, why do you think I set up all those Field Trips to the mayor's office? To get you and Ann together, of course.

But I forgive you!

Jack shook his head, exasperated.

By now you will have received the quilt I made for you, my son. I hope it brings you as much joy as it brought me creating it for you. You know how much I loved your father. My time with him was so fleeting, and I spent so many years alone mourning him.

DO NOT follow in my footsteps, Jack. You hear me?

Marry sweet Ann, find love as I had, and be happy for all your remaining years to come.

P.S. This is my last request, in case it wasn't obvious!

P.S.S. I will facilitate this from the grave ... and Alex will help.

—Your loving mother

Jack didn't know whether to be furious, laugh, or cry. And what on earth was he in store for, now that she would be facilitating his *third* marriage ... *from the grave?*

And was Alex in on this?

When he looked up from the letter, his eyes were on Alex, pleading for answers.

"I received the same type of letter, Jack," she said. "I had no idea what she was up to." She turned her head to meet eyes with Charlotte, who was desperately patting her letter with her sleeve to prevent her tears from staining the writing.

Alex handed Jack her letter to read as well. Once he finished reading Alex's letter, she handed him the envelope of cruise tickets.

157

"Why? How?" he questioned as he handed Alex's letter to Charlotte, and she began to read.

"Who is Henrietta?" Charlotte asked.

"Not who," Alex replied. "What. And the answer is—a quilt."

EPILOGUE

"There are two keys in here," Charlotte exclaimed, giving Alex a puzzled look. "Taped to the inside of the envelope with the tickets." Charlotte held up a grimy old skeleton key and an ordinary house key.

"The skeleton key looks like the one used to open the turret room door," Alex replied.

"Always cloak and dagger with Nona."

Alex and Charlotte tried the two keys everywhere they could and even searched the house for other doors, hidden boxes, secret panels, or secret rooms. The two searched number 9, Jack's house, where Nona had lived before moving into Alex's house. In a desperate attempt to make sense of it, they even tried the house key on everyone's doors in the neighborhood. Satisfied the keys did not belong to Spruce Street, Alex decided to bring them with her on the cruise.

Four months later, Alex breathed a sigh of relief, slipping her hand into her carry-on bag as she boarded the cruise ship *Tranquility*. Henrietta was neatly packed, along with the two keys, for the trip to their untold destination.

Ready to find out what happens next?

Buy Quilting Calamity - A Quilting Cozy Mystery
Book 2 in the Quilting Cozy Mysteries Series

Leave a review!

★ ★ ★ ★ ★
5 stars

"I'm going to share it with all my friends!"

"So much quilting goodness!"

**Thank you for reading my book!
I appreciate your feedback and love to hear about how you enjoyed it!**

Please leave a positive review letting me know what you thought.

THANK YOU! × × × ×

ABOUT THE AUTHOR

Inspired by the laugh-out-loud and fanciful aspects of cozies, Kathryn Mykel aims to write lighthearted, humorous cozies surrounding her passion for the craft of quilting.

Kathryn is an avid quilter and owner of a successful retail quilting business.

She was born and raised in a small New England town. She enjoys writing cozy mysteries and short 'mini mysteries'. You will find Kathryn has written a great howdunit where she weaves the plot through her characters and stitches together obscure clues and red herrings.

authorkathrynmykelsewingsuspicion.mailerpage.com

For more fun content and new releases, join Kathryn on Patreon, sign up for her newsletter, or join her and her thReaders on Facebook at Author Kathryn Mykel or Books For Quilters.

Printed in Great Britain
by Amazon

78327755R00098